"When I came back, I made a promise to myself that I wouldn't lean on anyone else. I would stand on my own two feet."

"Nothing wrong with that," Daniel said, "except that it's not the Amish way. We help one another, as you know very well. You wouldn't hesitate to help me if I needed it."

Rebecca's arguments were being cut from under her, and she struggled to find a solution they both could accept.

Daniel crossed the distance between them and stood smiling at her. "What's wrong? Can't find anything else to say?" His voice teased her gently.

"Suppose we do this. You let me help. Surely there are things I can do. And you don't turn down other jobs to work for me."

"Deal," Daniel said. He grinned at her. "See, that wasn't so hard, was it?"

She'd tell him it was, but he wouldn't understand. None of them would, because they didn't know what her life had been like with James.

She had to walk away from the past. She had to accept Daniel's help to do so. He held the door open to her new life, but she had to pass through, and she would.

A lifetime spent in rural Pennsylvania and her Pennsylvania Dutch heritage led **Marta Perry** to write about the Plain People who add so much richness to her home state. Marta has seen nearly sixty of her books published, with over six million books in print. She and her husband live in a centuries-old farmhouse in a central Pennsylvania valley. When she's not writing, she's reading, traveling, baking, or enjoying her six beautiful grandchildren.

Books by Marta Perry

Love Inspired

Brides of Lost Creek

Second Chance Amish Bride
The Wedding Quilt Bride

An Amish Family Christmas:
Heart of Christmas
Amish Christmas Blessings:
The Midwife's Christmas Surprise

Visit the Author Profile page at Harlequin.com for more titles.

The Wedding Quilt Bride

Marta Perry

HARLEQUIN® LOVE INSPIRED®

Recycling programs
for this product may
not exist in your area.

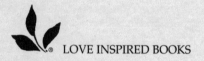 LOVE INSPIRED BOOKS

ISBN-13: 978-1-335-50946-8

The Wedding Quilt Bride

Copyright © 2018 by Martha Johnson

www.Harlequin.com

Printed in U.S.A.

Trust in the Lord with all thine heart;
and lean not unto thine own understanding.
In all thy ways acknowledge him,
and he shall direct thy paths.
—*Proverbs* 3:5–6

This story is dedicated to my husband, Brian,
with much love.

Chapter One

Two days after Rebecca Mast's return to her childhood home in Lost Creek, she walked down the lane of the family farm toward her future. Her black widow's dress contrasted starkly with the pale greens and bright yellows of a sunny spring day in the Pennsylvania countryside. Her son, six-year-old Elijah, trudged next to her, holding tight to her hand rather than skipping and hopping ahead down the lane like one of his cousins would.

It was early yet, she assured herself. Surely soon he'd forget the darkness of the past few years and be like any other Amish child his age. That was the heartfelt prayer of her heart for her son. As for her... well, the return to normal would take longer, if it ever happened.

But at least she was home, with her family around her, and today she would take the first step toward a new life for her son and herself. That alone was something to make her heart thankful.

The two-story frame house came into view ahead of them, standing at the point where the farm lane met the country road. When her mammi had written that old Mr. Evans had gone to live with his daughter and put the house up for sale, she'd known exactly what she wanted to do with the money she'd receive for selling the farm she and James had owned in Ohio.

The down payment James's brother, John, had given her had been enough to cover the cost of the house. John's continuing monthly payments would pay to remodel the old place into a secure, peaceful home for her and Elijah, and the quilt shop she'd have in the downstairs rooms would support them. That was the extent of her dreams for the future, and it was enough.

Daniel King stood, waiting by the back porch, leaning against one of the posts as if he could wait there all day for her, if need be. As they came closer, her stomach tightened as she searched the tall, broad figure for a glimpse of the neighbor boy who'd been her childhood playmate. She didn't find him, nor did she see the gangly teenager who'd told her all about his crushes on the girls in their rumspringa group.

Daniel had grown into a strong, sturdy-looking man. It was her own uncertainty that made her long to find something in him that was familiar. The rich, glossy brown of his hair was a bit darker now, and the fact that he didn't have the traditional Amish beard allowed her to see his stubborn jaw.

He'd always had that stubbornness. His golden-brown eyes had a glint of kindness that she felt sure reflected his kind heart, and his lips curled in a familiar grin. Her tension evaporated, and she smiled.

"Rebecca!" He came forward now to greet them, taking her hands in both of his for a momentary squeeze. "It's wonderful gut to see you again." His face sobered. "I'm sorry for your loss."

She nodded. She had a stock of reasonable comments to use when someone commented on her widowhood, but they didn't seem appropriate for Daniel, who'd known her so well.

Daniel didn't seem to notice. He'd focused on Lige, who was hiding behind her skirt, and he squatted down to eye level.

"You must be Elijah. I've heard about you from your grossmammi. She told me you just turned six. Is that right?"

Lige, clutching the fold of Rebecca's skirt, gave the smallest of nods. Fortunately, Daniel didn't seem to expect more.

"I'm Daniel," he said. "I live over there." He pointed across the field to the neighboring farm. "When your mammi and I were your age, we used to play together every day."

Still no response. She tried to think of something to say to pull his attention from Lige, but Daniel was already rising, his smile intact. "Ach, it's hard to get to know a lot of new folks at once, ain't so?"

"Yah, it is," she said, grateful for his understanding. "Sam tells me that your carpentry business is a wonderful success these days." Sam, Rebecca's older brother, had been best friends with Daniel's older brother, Caleb. It had seemed natural for her and Daniel to pair up, as well.

"Ach, I wouldn't say great, but it's doing okay. It doesn't give me much time to help Caleb with the dairy farm, but I do what I can. And he's got Onkel Zeb and young Thomas Stoltz to work with him, too."

"I'm sure he needs it, running such a big dairy operation." Daad had told her how Caleb had increased his herd until it was one of the larger ones in the valley. "I'd be most happy if you have time to take on this job for me."

She glanced at the house, trying to picture it the way it was in her dreams. With Daniel's help, that dream could be a reality.

"Let's go in and have a look at what you want done," Daniel suggested. He held out a hand as she reached the three steps up to the back porch. "Mind the treads, now. There's a loose board there I'll fix right off."

She nodded, turning to help Lige up to the porch. "It's a little bit run-down now," she told him. "But Daniel will help us turn it into a gut home for us."

Lige darted a cautious sideways glance at Daniel, but he still didn't speak. She tried to suppress a sigh. If she'd realized earlier the harm James's behavior was doing to Elijah…but what choice did she have? James had been his father, and there was no getting away from that.

The back door opened into the kitchen, and they stepped inside.

"The cabinets need some repair," Daniel said, swinging a door open and closed. "But they're good solid wood—none of those thin layers they use sometimes now."

Rebecca was busy picturing the kitchen with the cabinets freshly painted white and seedlings growing in pots on the wide, sunny windowsills. "The gas range is perfect," she said. "But I'll have to replace the electric refrigerator with a gas one."

"I don't know much about the electrics, but there's a man I worked with on a few Englisch houses who does that kind of work. He could take out all the electrics for you."

"Wonderful gut." Surely the fact that things were falling into place meant that her plans were in accord with the gut Lord's will. "Our table will fit in this space, won't it, Lige?"

He nodded but hadn't yet let go of her skirt.

"When do your things arrive?" Daniel pulled himself out from behind the refrigerator, a cobweb clinging to his straw hat.

"In a few days." Smiling, she reached up to lift the cobweb away, inadvertently brushing his cheek. She withdrew her hand quickly, trying to ignore the way it tingled from the brief contact. "The family will store everything for us until we can move in here."

The back of the house held the kitchen, a pantry and two smaller rooms. One would be their living room and the other a storeroom or workroom. Swinging the door open, Rebecca stepped into the room at the front of the house. Her breath caught.

The room extended across the whole front of the house, and sunshine poured in through the windows to lie across the wide-plank floors. The back wall would be perfect for shelves, and she could have a display area of quilts on one side and stocks of fabrics and notions on the other.

"You look happy," Daniel said, his brown eyes warm. "Is this going to be your living room?"

"No." She swung in a slow circle, taking it all in. "This will be what I've been dreaming of. This will be my quilt shop."

She knew her happiness had to be shining in her face. And when she looked at Daniel, she saw her anticipation reflected in his eyes, crinkling as they shared her feeling. There, at last, was her old friend.

Daniel stood still for a moment, transfixed by the sheer joy on Rebecca's face. He couldn't help but share it. Obviously, this quilt shop was important to her, but why? So far as he knew, she hadn't had a shop in the past.

He didn't doubt that she was a wonderful quilter. Rebecca's sister-in-law, Leah, had shown off the baby quilts Rebecca had made and sent for each of her young ones. Rebecca's mother had a gift for designing patterns, and she must have inherited it.

"Can you make this ready first?" She swung toward him, all eagerness. "I need to open the shop as soon as possible."

Need? That was a funny way of putting it. He'd heard that Rebecca sold the farm she and her husband had owned in Ohio. He'd think that would have given her enough that she wouldn't have to rush into business for herself.

Still, it might be that she felt she had to have something to occupy her mind and heart. Her husband had died less than six months ago, and grieving was hard—he knew that as well as anyone.

"I have plenty of time for your job," he said. And if he didn't, he'd make time to accommodate her, especially if it kept her looking the way she did now.

He couldn't deny that he'd been shocked when he first saw her, so thin and pale, with an almost-haunted look darkening the blue of her eyes. Rebecca had always been as bright as a ray of sunshine with her golden hair, rosy cheeks and the sparkle in her clear blue eyes. He nearly hadn't recognized his friend, and that had set a distance between them.

Already she was withdrawing into herself again, her face becoming strained. But at least now he'd seen the old Rebecca, if just for a moment.

"So, you'll tell me what you want done in here, and I'll do the measurements and work out a plan." He glanced toward the front door that led directly into the room. "We'd best check out the front entrance as well, if your customers are going to come in that way."

Rebecca nodded, looking around the room as if seeing it looking very different. "I'll want tables to hold bolts of fabric on this side," she said, gesturing. "And then some open space where I can have a bed to show how a quilt will look and a counter near the door for checking out."

Daniel made notes on his pad that no one would ever understand but him. "What about the walls?"

"They'll need to have several different-sized racks to hold quilts, crib quilts, wall hangings and table runners." She unfolded a sheet of paper, and they both bent their heads over it. "See, here are the kinds and sizes I need and where I thought maybe they could go."

She'd printed it all up for him with sketches. "So neat," he said. "Just like your schoolwork used to be." He glanced at the boy, standing quiet and solemn next to his mammi. Did he ever laugh? "When we were in school together, your mammi had the best printing of anyone in the school. Whenever a sign had to be made, we'd get her to do it."

Lige nodded, as if he didn't doubt it, but still he didn't smile or speak. Well, he'd get a smile out of the boy even if he had to stand on his head to do it.

He turned to Rebecca. It wouldn't be bad to get another smile from her, as well. "Do you want to make decisions about the rest of the house today, or just focus on the shop for now?"

"Just the shop today," she said quickly. "It's more important than getting moved in right away."

"If I know your mamm and daad, they'd be happy to have you stay with them in the grossdaadi house for always, ain't so?"

Her lips curved a bit, but her blue eyes were still dark and serious. "That's what they say, but we shouldn't impose on them."

Now all he could do was stare at her shuttered face. "Impose? Since when is it imposing to have you home again? Your folks have been so happy since they knew you were coming that they're acting ten years younger. Sam and Leah and their young ones have been marking the days off on a calendar because they're so eager. You're not imposing."

Rebecca stiffened, seeming to put some distance between them. "It's better that I stand on my own feet. I'm not a girl any longer." She looked as if she might want to add that it wasn't his business.

No, it wasn't. And she certain sure wasn't the girl he remembered. His Rebecca, so open and trusting, would never have doubted her welcome. Grief alone didn't seem enough to account for the changes in her. Had there been some other problem, something he didn't know about in her time away or in her marriage?

He'd best mind his tongue and keep his thoughts on business, he told himself. He was the last person to know anything about marriage, and that was the way he wanted it. Or if not wanted, he corrected himself honestly, at least the way it had to be.

"I guess we should get busy measuring for all these things, so I'll know what I'm buying when I go to the mill." Pulling out his steel measure, he focused on the boy. "Mind helping me by holding one end of this, Lige?"

The boy hesitated for a moment, studying him as if looking at the question from all angles. Then he nodded, taking a few steps toward Daniel, who couldn't help feeling a little spurt of triumph.

Carefully, not wanting to spook Lige, Daniel held out an end of the tape. "If you'll hold this end right here on the corner, I'll measure the whole wall. Then we can see how many racks we'll be able to put up."

Rebecca, who had taken a step forward as if to interfere, stopped and nodded at her son. "That's right. You can help with getting our shop ready."

Daniel measured, checking a second time before writing the figures down in his notebook. His gaze slid toward Lige again. It wondered him how the boy came to be so quiet and solemn. He certain sure wasn't like his mammi had been when she was young. Could be he was still having trouble adjusting to his daadi's dying, he supposed.

"Okay, gut. Now, you let the end go, and I'll show you how it pops back to me. Ready?" Lige put his end on the floor and took a cautious step away, as if not sure what to expect.

"Now." Daniel pushed the button, and the steel measure came zooming back, rerolling itself. "There. Did you ever use one of these before?"

Lige shook his head and hurried over to Daniel without hesitation. "Can we do it some more?"

"Sure thing. Let's measure how wide the window is, because we wouldn't want a quilt to cover it, would we?"

Without being told, Lige pulled the end out so that they could measure the width of the windowsill. When they'd finished, Daniel held out the tape measure to the boy. "Do you want to roll it up this time?"

Lige came eagerly, his shyness of Daniel forgotten. Daniel put his large hand over the boy's small one, showing him the button. "Now, push."

Lige did, and the tape measure performed its vanishing trick again. He looked up at Daniel, and the sight Daniel had been looking for appeared. It was tentative and a little stiff, but it was a genuine smile.

"Did you see, Mammi? I did it all by myself."

"Yah, I saw." Some of the color had come back into Rebecca's pale cheeks, and she met Daniel's gaze with one that was so filled with fierce maternal love that it startled him. "Denke, Daniel."

He shrugged. "It's nothing."

Somehow that simple incident seemed to dissolve much of the strangeness between them. They worked their way around the room, measuring and talking about what she wanted in the shop, until finally Daniel squatted down and put his notebook on his knee to figure out an estimate.

He stole a covert glance at Rebecca, who was saying something to her son. He hadn't missed the slight apprehension in her face when he'd talked about the supplies they'd need. Was the money a problem?

It shouldn't be, not if she'd just sold a thriving farm,

but how did he know? He'd do the work gladly for nothing in the name of their old friendship, but he knew Rebecca wouldn't hear of it. That steely independence of hers was new, and he wasn't sure how to handle it.

Finally he had an approximate materials cost worked out. He stood, catching that trace of apprehension in her eyes.

"How much will it cost to do what I want?"

In answer, he held out the notebook page. "That's an approximate guess as to the cost of the materials. Unless the mill has upped its prices for a board foot," he said. "Just joking," he added quickly, not sure she was in the mood for humor.

"But that's not including your work," she said. "I should give you the whole amount…"

"Not up front," he said, interrupting her. "You pay for the initial materials, so I can start. Then you can pay my labor when the job is finished." Seeing the objection rising in her face, he added firmly, "That's how it's always done, Rebecca. If that outlay for materials is more than you can manage at one time, we can always break the job into smaller units."

"No, no, that's okay." She opened a small bag and began counting out the money into his hand.

He didn't miss the fact that there was very little left in the bag when she was done, and it troubled him. But when she looked up at him with the smile he remembered, it chased other thoughts away.

"I'll go to the mill first thing tomorrow, and then I can start work in the afternoon." He glanced at Lige. "You'll bring my helper back, ain't so?"

The boy's smile rewarded him. "Can I, Mammi?" He tugged on her apron.

"Yah, as long as you listen to Daniel and do just as he says."

"I will. I promise."

"Sehr gut," Daniel said. "Tomorrow then." Shouldering his tool bag, he headed out.

Rebecca and her son followed him to the porch and stood there, watching him go. As he cut across the field toward home, he took a quick look back and again was assailed by that sense of something he didn't understand. The two of them looked oddly lonely, standing there on the porch of that decrepit house.

Rebecca was home, but he sensed she had brought some troubles with her. As for him…well, he didn't have answers. He just had a lot of questions.

Supper in Leah's kitchen was a lively time, with the long table surrounded by cheerful faces—Leah, Sam, their children, her mamm and daad, and now her and Lige. Lige, sitting next to her, had been engrossed in looking from one to another during the meal, his small face gradually relaxing as he realized all the chatter was normal and accepted.

It had been normal when she was growing up, as well. It never would have occurred to any of her siblings that their contributions wouldn't be welcome. But life with James, especially after his accident, had been another story entirely.

At least Lige was beginning to lose the tension that told her so clearly he was waiting for an explosion. He actually laughed at something one of his cousins said, and she breathed a silent prayer of thanks.

With the last crumb of apple crisp consumed and the silent prayer at the end of the meal said, the boys began getting up from the table to do their chores. Sam, who'd been saying something to Daad, glanced up as they headed out the door.

"Joshua." He raised his voice to call his eldest back.

And Lige cringed, wincing back in his chair, his face strained and fearful.

No one moved. Rebecca could hear their indrawn breaths, could see the comprehension dawning on the faces of the adults. Rebecca bent over Lige, speaking softly.

"Hush now. It's all right. Onkel Sam just wants to tell Joshua something."

Leah seemed to get a grip on herself first. "Yah, he wants to tell Joshua to take Lige out with him and let him help. Ain't so, Sam?"

"For sure," Sam said.

Kindhearted Joshua came and squatted down by Lige's seat. "Want to komm help me feed the buggy horses? You can measure the oats, yah?" He spoke softly, holding out his hand to Lige.

Lige looked up at her, as if asking for guidance.

"You'll like that," she said, flashing a glance of thanks to her nephew. "Go along with Joshua and the other boys now."

Lige slid off his chair, probably glad to get out of the kitchen. He took Joshua's hand, and they went off together.

At a look from Leah, Sam and Daad went out, too.

"You girls make a start on the dishes now," she said. "I want to show your aunt Rebecca some of my quilts."

"Yah, you go on," Mamm added. "I'll look after things here."

Mamm was obviously trying hard to erase the shock from her face. Maybe she needed time as much as Rebecca did just now.

Leah ushered Rebecca into the sewing room and opened a trunk to reveal the quilts inside. "You don't have to look at these now," she said. "I just thought you might want a reason to be by yourself for a minute."

"Denke," she murmured, feeling the blood mounting to her cheeks. "It must wonder you why…"

Leah touched her hand. "You don't need to explain anything. But when you do want to talk, I'm here and ready to listen." Leah put her arms around her for a quick, strong embrace. "I'm your sister now, ain't so?" she murmured.

It was a struggle to hold back tears. Maybe it would be a relief to talk, but not now, not when the emotions were still raw, even after months.

"I'll check on the girls," Leah said, seeming to understand. "You take as long as you want." She slipped out quickly.

Alone, Rebecca slid down on the floor next to the trunk, her hand resting on the Sunshine and Shadows quilt that lay on top. Sunshine and Shadows, she repeated silently. There had been mostly shadows for so long. She longed to believe the sunshine was coming back to their lives.

As for talking about it…how could she tell anyone? Mamm and Daadi hadn't wanted her to marry James so quickly, to go so far away with someone they barely knew. But she'd been captivated by James's charm and his lively, daring personality.

She didn't know then about the quick temper that seemed to be a part of him. It had flared rarely in the first years of their marriage, and each time it did, she'd made excuses for him.

And then had come the accident. James's daring had led him a little too far, determined to climb to the top of the windmill to repair it, unwilling to wait for someone to come help him. And annoyed with her when she tried to stop him.

So she'd stood, watching, wondering what made him so eager to take risks. Then... Her memory winced away from the image of him falling, falling...

Everyone, even the doctors, said he was fortunate to be alive. That his injuries would heal, and he'd be himself again.

But he wasn't. After the injury to his head, James seemed to lose all control. His rages were terrifying. If she dared try to calm him, he'd turn on her. Lige had become a little mouse, always afraid, trying so hard not to do anything to bring on the anger. And she hadn't been much better.

Until the day he'd almost struck Lige with his fist. Then she had found the courage to fight back. When his family seemed unable to help, she'd dared to go to the bishop.

Bishop Paul had been everything that was kind. He'd insisted that James go for treatment, making all the arrangements himself. For a time, the treatment helped. The rages became a thing of the past, and it had seemed a blessing to be able to hope again.

Then it had all fallen apart. James had lost his temper with a half-trained horse, determined to force it to obey. The animal had reared, striking out, and in a moment, James was gone.

Rebecca pressed her fingers to her eyes, willing the images away. James was gone, but the damage he'd done lived on after him, it seemed.

No. She forced herself to stand, to wipe the tears from her face. That was the past. It was over and done with. She and Lige had a new start here, and they would make the best of it. But she would never again make the mistake of trusting a man with their lives.

Chapter Two

When Daniel turned into the lane and drew the horse to a halt at the back door of Rebecca's new house, the troubling thoughts about her returned in full force. Onkel Zeb, sitting next to him on the wagon seat, started to get down and then looked at him.

"Was ist letz? Is something wrong?"

"No, no." He secured the lines and scolded himself for daydreaming. "It's nothing. I can unload myself, if you have something else to do." He'd appreciated the company on the trip to the hardware store and lumber-yard for the materials he'd need for Rebecca's job, but he didn't want to keep his uncle working all day.

Onkel Zeb, as lean and tough as he always was, hopped down nimbly. "Nothing as interesting as this," he said, heading for the back of the wagon. "I want to see what you and Rebecca are going to do to this place. Mason Evans let it go those last few years, that's certain sure."

"He didn't seem to have much energy for it after his wife passed, did he? But we'll get it fixed up fine." He slid a couple of two-by-fours off the wagon and balanced them on his shoulder. "If you'll get the door, I'll take the bigger pieces in. Rebecca said she'd leave it unlocked for us."

Nodding, Zeb stepped up to the porch and swung the door open. "I was hoping Rebecca would be here when we got back. I haven't seen her yet. How is she looking?"

Daniel moved past him to start a stack of the lumber inside while he considered how to answer that question. "All right, I guess," he muttered.

His uncle propped the door open before turning to give him a probing look. "Seems to me you're not so sure about that, ain't so?"

He should have known there was no getting away with evasions where Onkel Zeb was concerned. He'd been like a father to all three boys, especially after their mother left and their own daad just seemed to fall apart at the loss.

Don't go down that road, he told himself. *This is about Rebecca, not you.*

"Truth to tell, I'm not sure." He pulled another couple of posts out and hesitated. "She's so thin and pale I almost didn't know her. It's not so long since her husband died, so I guess that's natural, but…"

"But what?" Onkel Zeb leaned against the buggy, ready to listen as always.

Daniel frowned absently at the boards. "Seemed like her whole personality has changed from what she was. She was all tense and keyed up, and the boy… He seemed almost scared."

"Of you?"

Daniel shrugged. "Maybe. Or maybe of everything. Just didn't seem right." He eyed his uncle thoughtfully.

"You and Josiah Fisher are pretty close. He say anything to you about Rebecca?"

Onkel Zeb hesitated so long Daniel thought he wasn't going to answer. Finally he spoke. "Josiah and Ida have been worried about Rebecca for a while now, her being so far away that they couldn't help as much as they wanted when she had all this trouble."

That wasn't really an answer, and they both knew it. "So why did they start worrying to begin with?"

"What do you remember about when Rebecca got married?" Onkel Zeb answered the question with a question.

Daniel cast his mind back. "I remember she went away that summer—out to Ohio to help a cousin of hers who was moving. She stayed quite a time, and then we heard she'd met someone and was going to marry him." He rubbed the back of his neck. "Funny. We'd always been such gut friends, but she didn't write to me about him at all."

"That was the summer you were chasing after Betty Ann Stoltzfus," Onkel Zeb put in. "Maybe you were too busy to pay much attention to what Rebecca was up to."

Daniel had a moment's gratitude for the fact that he'd broken it off with Betty Ann when he did. They wouldn't have suited anyway, and it was not long afterward that his little brother, Aaron, took off for the Englisch world, tearing up his heart.

Onkel Zeb made a sound that expressed his general disapproval of Betty Ann. "Anyway, Josiah and Ida didn't want her to get married so quick, especially to someone they hardly knew, who lived so far away. But she was determined, so they accepted the best they could."

"Rebecca being the only daughter, I guess it's natural they'd want her to stay close." He picked up another armload of planks. It had begun to sound as if Onkel Zeb was doing a good bit of talking around the subject, maybe not wanting to repeat anything Josiah said about his daughter in confidence.

"Yah." Zeb slid out some of the smaller pieces and a box of nails and followed him to the house. "Natural, like you say. They always thought maybe you and Rebecca would make a match of it, as close as you were."

That startled him. He'd never imagined anyone could be thinking that. "We were friends, that's all," he said quickly. "Neither of us ever thought of anything else."

There was a skeptical expression on Onkel Zeb's lean, lined face, but he didn't argue. Instead, he turned back toward the door. "I'll bring the rest of the small stuff in."

He'd need the sawhorses and his tools, but for a moment, Daniel stood where he was, processing that idea. All he could think now was that it had been fortunate he and Rebecca hadn't been more than friends. He wouldn't have wanted to let her down.

It wouldn't have to be that way. The small voice of hope spoke in his head, but he squashed it. Maybe it didn't have to be, but it was. After all, it had happened before. When Mamm left…

He'd been the closest to their mother of the three boys. So close he'd always thought he even knew what she was thinking. But he hadn't. She must have been unhappy for a long time to run away to the Englisch world and leave them behind. And he'd never seen it. If he had, he might have made a difference.

Logic might say that a ten-year-old couldn't influence what a grown woman did, but somehow Daniel didn't believe in logic when he thought about running upstairs to Mammi's bedroom to tell her about the good grade he'd got on his spelling test, only to discover that the room was empty of everything that belonged to her. Everything except the letter that lay on the pillow, addressed to Daad. Nothing for him, her favorite.

There had been times when he'd nearly run off to try to find her. And worse times when he didn't know whether it was worth it to go on living. Daad, shattered himself, hadn't been any help. They'd never have got through it without Onkel Zeb.

And then, just when Daniel had begun thinking that losing Mamm that way hadn't tainted him forever, Aaron had left. Little Aaron, the baby brother he'd always looked after, taken care of, defended. He'd told himself taking care of Aaron was his job—maybe he'd even taken pride in how close they were.

But he'd failed Aaron, too. He hadn't known that the forces of rebellion were growing so fiercely in Aaron that he'd pack up and leave. Like Mammi, except that Aaron hadn't even left a note.

Daniel had understood then. He couldn't be trusted not to fail the people he loved. So he certain sure couldn't take the risk of letting a wife and children depend on him.

Onkel Zeb clattered back in with another armload. "You want to help me with the sawhorses?"

"Yah, sorry. I'll get them." Daniel shook off his

mood. No sense reliving the past. This was now, and there was work to be done.

But when they pulled the last few things off the wagon, it was Onkel Zeb who paused, his thoughts clearly far away.

"You know something more about Rebecca," Daniel said, knowing it was so. He waited. Was he going to hear what it was?

"I can't tell you all of it," his uncle said, continuing the conversation that was on both their minds. "Parts I don't know, and parts Josiah most likely wouldn't want repeated." His solemn gaze met Daniel's. "But I do know that Rebecca has seen more trouble than most folks twice her age. And right now, what she needs most is a friend." He paused, and Daniel thought for a moment that he was praying. "You can be that friend she needs, Daniel. If you will."

"Yah, for sure." He didn't need to know any details to promise that, but his heart was chilled, nonetheless. "I've always been Rebecca's friend, and I always will be."

By the next day, Rebecca had begun to feel that, aside from a few bumps in the road, Lige was doing better each day. And if he was, that meant she could be happier, as well. She and Leah were doing the breakfast dishes together after the younger children had left for school, and Leah's sunny kitchen seemed to hold the echo of the kinder's chatter and laughter.

"Come September, your Lige will be joining the other scholars on their way to school," Leah commented. "He'll like it, I'm sure. Teacher Esther is wonderful gut with the kinder."

"It's hard to believe my little one is that old. I'll miss him." Rebecca's smile was tinged with a little regret. In a normal Amish family, Lige would have been joined by a couple of younger siblings by now.

"You won't miss him as much as you think." Leah's tone was practical. "By then, your quilt shop will be thriving, and you'll have plenty to keep you busy."

"I hope so." Rebecca breathed a silent prayer.

"I was thinking about the shop," Leah said. "How would it be if I asked some of the other women to bring in quilts on consignment? I know several fine quilters who would like a regular store to sell their goods, instead of relying on mud sales and the like."

Rebecca blinked. It seemed Leah was thinking ahead even more than she had. "That's a grand idea, for sure. I'd love it. Do you really think they would? I've been away so long that they probably feel they hardly know me by now."

"Ach, that doesn't make a bit of difference. Folks remember you. You'd be doing a gut thing for them. And then there are some women like Martha Miller. She doesn't get around much now, but she'd love to do more sewing for folks. You could get her some work by letting customers know that she does hand quilting."

"Yah, I could." Excitement began to bubble. "I could have a bulletin board, maybe, where I could post things like that for customers to see. Denke, Leah. You…" Her throat tightened. "I'm sehr glad Sam had enough sense to marry you. I couldn't ask for a better sister."

Leah clasped Rebecca's hand with her soapy one.

"Ach, it's nothing. We're wonderful glad you've come home."

The back screen door closed softly, and Rebecca turned to smile at her son. It had to be Lige, because any of the others would have let the door bang.

"Mammi, can't we go yet? Daniel is counting on me to help."

"In a few minutes, Lige. I'll be out as soon as I'm ready."

He looked disappointed, but he didn't argue. Sometimes she almost wished he would. Instead, he slipped quietly out again.

A silence fell between her and Leah, making her wonder if Leah was thinking the same thing.

"That Daniel," Leah said. "The kinder are all crazy about him. It's a shame he doesn't have a passel of little ones of his own by this time."

"I've thought that, too," Rebecca admitted. "I kept expecting to hear he'd been married, but it didn't happen."

"No." Leah shook her head. "I hope he wasn't listening to that foolish talk that went around after Caleb's first wife left him. Folks saying that history was repeating itself, and that the King men couldn't find happiness in marriage."

"That's not just foolish, it's downright wrong. Just because of their mother, and then Caleb's wife…" Rebecca was too indignant to find the right words. "Anyway, with Caleb happily married now, surely that shows they were wrong."

"Yah, you'd think so, wouldn't you?" Leah dumped the dishwater and dried her hands. "But it's hard to know what Daniel is thinking sometimes. He took it awful hard when Aaron jumped the fence."

"He would," Rebecca said, her heart aching for Daniel's little brother, out there in the Englisch world somewhere. "Daniel always felt responsible for Aaron, especially after their mother left. He…"

Whatever she might have said was lost in the noise as a large truck came down the lane. Leah craned her neck to see out the window.

"It's the moving truck," she exclaimed. "Your things are here!"

Together they hurried outside, and Rebecca felt her heart beat a little faster. Her belongings—the furniture she'd wanted to bring, Lige's toys, her collection of quilts—they were finally here. Now she could start to feel at home.

When they reached the rear of the truck, the driver was opening the door and letting down the ramp. Almost before he'd finished, the rest of the family had arrived—her mother and father from the grossdaadi house, Sam and the older boys from the barn and the eldest girl from the chicken coop. She even spotted Daniel hastening down the lane toward them.

Mamm put her arm around Rebecca's waist. "Now you'll start to feel settled, ain't so? You're really home." Her eyes clouded over with tears, making Rebecca wonder how much Mamm had been worrying about her.

"I'll need to sort things…" she began, and Daad interrupted before she could head into the van.

"All you have to do is say where each thing goes as we bring it off. Someone will carry it there." Daad's voice didn't allow an argument.

But still she felt vaguely guilty, drawing them all away from the things they'd been doing.

"Furniture in our basement for now," Leah said. "It's all cleaned and ready. Just pick out what you want in the grossdaadi house. You won't want anything to go in your new place yet, ain't so?"

Rebecca shook her head. "It would just be in Daniel's way."

"That's right," Daniel said, tapping Lige's straw hat. "We men need to have room to work, ain't so, Lige?"

Her son nodded, his smile chasing any tension from his face.

The next few minutes were a scramble, as things started coming out of the van so fast that it was all she could do to keep up. Lige showed a tendency to want to open boxes to see what was inside, until Daniel showed him how they were marked.

Sam marshaled his young ones into a line. He picked up each item in turn, checked with Rebecca what she wanted done with it and then gave it to one of the kinder to hurry off with. Daniel came out balancing several large boxes and headed for her.

"My quilts!" Her heart seemed to lurch with excitement. There they were, all packed up, the things that would allow her to support herself and her son.

Daniel's grin said he understood, at least a little, what this meant to her. "Should we toss these in the chicken coop?" he said, teasing her the way he'd teased the girl she used to be.

"Into my sewing room," Leah said firmly. "I don't need the space just now, and they'll be handy for you there."

Joshua, Leah's eldest, seized the boxes from Daniel.

"I've got it, Mammi." He strode toward the back door, Lige scurrying ahead to hold the door open for him.

They'd left Rebecca nothing to do but watch as the van emptied and Leah produced coffee and crullers for the driver. "I hate to put everyone to so much trouble," Rebecca murmured. "I shouldn't…"

"Ach, don't be foolish." Daniel gave her a friendly nudge. "Look at them. See how happy they are? It would be wrong to take away their joy in doing something for you."

All of her arguments about standing on her own feet and taking care of herself and her son seemed useless against Daniel's perceptive comment. She glanced at him. He was right, and his smile said he knew it.

Maybe she should argue, but she was too happy just now to care.

Chapter Three

Rebecca walked into the shop the next morning to hear the sound of a saw. Obviously, Daniel was already at work, and that gave a boost to her already-optimistic frame of mind. She hadn't realized how much it would mean to have her own belongings here with her and Lige.

Maybe every mother had these strong instincts to create a nest for her family. With their own things surrounding them, she and Lige could feel at home. And how much better it would be when this place was finished. She looked around the kitchen, seeing it not as it was, but as it would be, with the gas appliances, the pie cabinet she'd inherited from her grandmother, her dishes on the shelves and pots of herbs growing on the windowsills.

But there was work to be done, and dreaming wouldn't get it accomplished. Rebecca headed into the front room.

Daniel looked up from the sawhorses with a warm smile. "You're here, but where is my helper?"

"He'll be along in a minute. He's been begging to

be allowed to bring the mail from the box, so I said he could today." She could see him now through the front window, skirting along the edge of the road toward the box.

"Lige will be fine," Daniel said, apparently reading her thoughts. "He's growing a little every day. Like you did at that age." He grinned. "That was when you started wearing your braids pinned up under your kapp, remember?"

"I remember thinking it was a gut idea, because then you and the other boys couldn't pull my braids," she said with mock tartness. "You were a bunch of little monsters at that age."

"Were not," he said quickly, just as he would have all those years ago. Then he turned back to his work, measuring a board he'd laid out. "Funny thing," he said.

"What's funny?" She bent to pick up the pencil he'd dropped just as he reached for it.

"I'm just thinking that with gut friends, you can pick up just where you left off, no matter how many years it's been in between."

Rebecca was speechless for a moment. Sometimes it seemed she was looking at Daniel with new eyes, seeing things she hadn't noticed before. "Yah, that's true, I think. When did you get so wise? You didn't show any signs of that when you were little."

"What kid does?" he asked. "It takes a bit of living to find some qualities in yourself. And maybe some folks never find them."

Could he be right? If so, then she might have had the seeds within her the whole time to bear the burden of James's injury and the effect it had had on their marriage. It wasn't anything she'd ever expected.

She shook herself out of her momentary absorption, not wanting Daniel to think he'd made her sorrowful. "I certain sure never showed much sign of wisdom myself. Like the time I tried to prove that I could climb higher in the willow tree than Sam, and got stuck there. And all Sam could do was stand there and say he'd told me not to do it."

"Sam was the one who wasn't smart," he said, grinning. "We knew how strong-willed you were. Telling you not to was the surest way to get you to do it."

"I can still remember how small he was when I looked down at him from above. It would have been a triumph if I hadn't outsmarted myself by going too far to get down."

"You did get back to the ground, though. And you managed it without falling on your head." He marked the board with care.

"Only because you talked me through it, climbing up to me and showing me exactly where to put my hands and feet so I could get safely down."

"That was my strength," he said, his grin smug. "I could talk you into things. Did I ever tell you I was scared stiff you were going to fall and Onkel Zeb would blame me? I had a lot to lose if I didn't get you down."

"I should have known there was something in it for you. Just like the day you talked me into sneaking one of Mammi's cherry pies. I'll never forget how you looked when Mammi caught us with cherry all over our faces."

They were both laughing at the image when Lige

came in, the mail clutched against his chest with both hands. He looked from one to the other, his eyes wide. Most likely, he didn't expect grown-ups to behave that way.

Rebecca swallowed her laughter. "Ach, Lige must think we're crazy." She smiled at her son. "It's a funny story about something we did when we were little. I'll tell you about it later," she said. "You can go ahead and run the mail to Aunt Leah, and then come back and help."

"There is one for you, Mammi." Lige extracted it carefully from the bunch. "I'm delivering it first. Now I'll take the rest, and then I'll come back and help Daniel, yah?"

She had to smile at his solemn attitude toward his new responsibilities. "Sehr gut. Denke, Lige."

With a quick smile for Daniel, he hurried off with the mail, his shoulders squared with responsibility.

When he'd gone, Rebecca turned her attention to the envelope in her hand. It was from John, James's brother, so it must mean that he'd sent the amount of his first monthly payment. Relief washed through her. Thank the good Lord it was here. She'd been running low on cash, and she wouldn't feel right asking her parents for help. They'd done enough for her already.

Ripping it open, she looked for the pale blue check that was sure to be enclosed. But it wasn't. There was just a letter from John, brief and to the point. He couldn't pay her now. No excuses, no reason. Just a short statement.

She stared at the page, her body rigid while her mind raced. What was she going to do? How could John do this to them?

* * *

Daniel, watching her, saw the color drain from Rebecca's face as she stared at the letter she'd received. His stomach clenched into a knot. She looked worse now than she had on the first day after she'd come back.

He dropped the tape measure. "Rebecca, was ist letz? Is it bad news you got?"

As if suddenly aware of his presence, Rebecca spun away from him, turning her back. Shutting him out. He had a brief flare of totally inappropriate anger.

Her hand, still holding the paper, was trembling, and sympathy washed away the anger in an instant.

"I can see it's bad news." He kept his voice gentle. "Won't you tell me what it is?"

"It's…it's nothing," she said, but her voice and her body gave the lie to the words.

"It's something," he said, propelled by the need to help close the distance between them, but not quite daring to touch her. "Trouble shared is trouble halved, ain't so?"

Rebecca turned to face him. For an instant, he thought she'd burst out with it, but then he saw that her lips were folded tightly together.

His jaw tightened in response as he took in that refusal. "Remember what I was saying about friendship never changing? It looks as if I was wrong, yah?"

For an instant, she glared at him, and he thought she was going to walk out. Then she sucked in a deep breath. "I… I'm sorry if it seemed that way. This affects you, so I guess you'll have to know anyway."

He wanted to reach out and touch her, but instinct

told him it wouldn't be welcome. Instead, he waited, sure now that she'd tell him, whatever it was.

Rebecca gave a sidelong look at the letter, almost as if she needed to avoid it. "The note is from my brother-in-law, John. The one who is buying the farm in Ohio from me."

She seemed to have difficulty getting the words out, and he tried to help her along. "Yah, I know. You mentioned that you'd used his down payment to buy this house."

"I did. And his monthly payments were intended to cover the costs of remodeling and getting my business started. The first one should have come by today." The hand holding the letter trembled again before she saw and seemed to force it to steady. "But he says he can't make the payment this month. He'll send it later."

Daniel frowned, trying to make sense of it. "But… does he say why?"

"No. No explanation. But then, John's not one to explain himself." She rubbed her arms, almost as if she was cold.

He was beginning to form a picture in his mind of the brother-in-law, and it wasn't a very complimentary one. What was the man about, to fail in his duty to his dead brother's widow and child?

"Did you have a written contract with him?" It wasn't his business, but he hoped now that she was talking, she'd keep going.

"Yah. I maybe wouldn't have thought of it, but Daad was there at the time, and he insisted a written contract was proper. I think James's family was a little offended by his attitude, but Daadi wouldn't let it go." She might have seen his surprise that she'd even let her father handle the negotiations, because she made a small movement with her hands, as if pushing something away. "Daad and Mammi gave us money to help buy the farm to begin with, so it only seemed right for him to have a say in what happened."

Thank the good Lord that Josiah had such a businesslike attitude toward it. Folks didn't usually get the better of a hardheaded Pennsylvania Dutchman easily.

"Seems like it was smart you listened to him. At least you have it in writing." He hesitated and then said what was in his mind. "Maybe you should remind John of that contract he signed." He was probably going too far, but Rebecca seemed to need bolstering up where her in-laws were concerned.

He wasn't sure she took in what he said, but finally she shook her head. "No. There's nothing I can do. I don't want to start a hassle with James's family."

"Seems to me John is the one who started it."

She just looked at him, and he knew what she was thinking. Finally he shrugged, his palms up. "Yah, all right, I know. It's not my business. I just don't like to see him take advantage of you."

"I'll handle it." Rebecca retreated into herself. Clearly, she had nothing else to say.

He had a few more arguments he'd like to express, but he restrained himself. Turning back to his work, he had to start again with the measurements, having totally forgotten what he'd come up with. It didn't help that he watched Rebecca covertly all the time he was doing it.

She might not be talking, but her body language was clear enough, with that stiff back and tight face.

Why was she so determined to handle everything on her own? It wasn't natural in an Amish family, where helping each other was considered God's plan, and that sort of independence drew very near to pride, about the worst thing for an Amish person. But if he said *that* to her, she'd probably never speak to him again.

Finally Rebecca seemed to pull herself out of her worried thoughts. She moved toward him, so he looked up from his work, and his heart twisted. Rebecca looked as if she were picking up a burden that was too heavy for her.

"You'll have to stop work." She blurted the words out and then sucked in a breath. "I'm sorry. This isn't fair to you, but…"

"We talked about this." His voice might be calm, but his thoughts were spinning rapidly, trying to come up with a way to change her mind. "You have already paid for the materials, and you don't owe me anything until the job is finished. Surely by then your brother-in-law will have paid what he owes you."

Rebecca's hands clung to each other until the knuckles were white. "That would not be fair. I can't accept your work when I don't know when or if I'll have the money to pay you."

"Ach, Rebecca, I would do the work for nothing for an old friend. The money doesn't matter."

"It matters to me," she snapped. "I won't accept charity."

"Charity?" He straightened, his own temper finally flaring, although he wasn't sure whom he was angrier at, Rebecca or that brother-in-law of hers. "Who's talking about charity? The Fishers and the Kings have been doing things for each other for a hundred years.

Seems to me your time away from here has made you forget a lot of things. It's made you prideful."

He shouldn't have said that, but he could be just as determined as she could. Rebecca might have been able to push him into a mud puddle once and not have him shove back, but she wasn't going to push him around now.

Rebecca's face had tightened into a mask that bore little resemblance to the girl she'd been. "Prideful or not, this is my decision. And my house. Please put down your tools and stop. Now."

"And when Lige comes back ready to help me? How are you going to explain that to him?"

"Lige is my son. I'll tell him what he needs to hear."

Daniel stared at her for a long minute, trying to make sense of her attitude. He couldn't.

"If you reject my help, Rebecca, you are rejecting our friendship."

He knew he shouldn't have said it the instant the words were out, but it was too late. Rebecca took a step away from him. She crossed her arms.

"Please go, Daniel."

There was nothing for it but to pick up his tool bag and leave, berating himself the whole time for handling her so badly. And yet, what else could he have done?

The trouble was that he kept thinking he knew her, and maybe he was wrong. Maybe he didn't know Rebecca at all.

Rebecca didn't look forward to telling Lige that the project was off and he wouldn't be working with Daniel for now. She waited until they were walking back to the farmhouse, thinking it would be easier away from the place he connected with Daniel. It would hurt, but she assumed he'd take it as silently as he did everything else.

But in this, she was wrong. To her astonishment, her quiet little son started to argue with her. Lige, who never spoke up for himself, was actually disagreeing.

"But, Mammi, you can't do that. Daniel wants to work on the shop with me. You can't!" He tugged on her apron, as if that would make her see reason.

She stared at him, trying to gather her wits. "I'm sorry, Lige. I know you're disappointed, but that's how it is right now. When I can afford to pay Daniel, he'll come back. You'll see."

"But I want to work with him now." It was almost a wail. "Won't he come back now if you ask him?"

Rebecca bit her tongue to keep from saying something that would put the blame on Daniel. She couldn't be that unjust to him, even if it were easier on her. "Daniel is willing, but it wouldn't be fair. Carpentry is how he makes his living. He has to be free to accept jobs for people who can pay."

Lige's lower lip came out in a decided pout. "He'd rather work for us. I know. We make him smile."

"Daniel is friendly. He smiles at everyone."

"Not like that. Please, Mammi. Please, please, please."

Her father came around the house in time to hear Lige's words, and his face crinkled. "It sounds as if this boy really wants something. What is it, Lige? A cookie?"

Lige shook his head. "Mammi says Daniel can't work for us anymore because we don't have money to pay him. But Daniel would, wouldn't he? You tell her, Grossdaadi."

Her father's gaze studied her face, and she longed to turn away but couldn't. Daadi touched Lige's cheek lightly. "I'll tell you what. You go and help Grossmammi with the cookies she's making, and I'll talk to your mamm."

"Snickerdoodles?" Lige asked hopefully. At his grandfather's nod, he darted off, leaving Rebecca to face what would probably be a lecture.

"Let's sit down on the steps."

She wanted to argue, but she couldn't. Daadi led her to the porch steps and waited while she took a seat.

"I know what you're going to say, but I don't want you to pay Daniel. I need to do this by myself. Don't you see?"

"No. I don't." Her father didn't scold. Instead, he seemed disappointed. "Did John Mast not send the money he owes?"

She shook her head. "He wrote and said he couldn't right now. The point is that I can't let Daniel keep working if I can't pay him. It wouldn't be right."

"What did Daniel say to that?"

"He offered to keep on working." She evaded his steady gaze.

"How did you convince him to stop, then?"

She'd never doubted her father's wisdom. He could go straight to the heart of what his children weren't saying to him. "I…I said something that hurt his feelings. But it wasn't all my fault. He was the one who…"

Rebecca let that trail off, because it was starting to sound like her explanations of the quarrels she'd had with her brothers when they were small.

Daadi gave her a disappointed look. "He is your friend, Rebecca. I shouldn't have to tell you what you must do when you've hurt a friend."

She wanted to argue, but she couldn't think of a thing to say. Daniel shouldn't have pushed her into that position. But she certain sure should have found a way of dealing with him that didn't involve causing him pain.

Sitting there debating with herself wasn't getting her anywhere. She didn't have to let Daniel continue to work for her, but she did have to ask his forgiveness for her anger. She pushed herself to her feet.

"You will find Daniel in his workshop," Daadi said calmly. "I saw him go in a few minutes ago."

Rebecca headed reluctantly toward the King place. She should have hired someone she didn't know to do the work for her, she thought rebelliously. Then she wouldn't have been put in this position.

Daniel's shop was a square-frame building situated at a little distance from the barns. Daad had told her that he'd built up quite a business for himself in the past couple of years, even doing some kitchen remodeling for a few Englisch families. Daniel was a hard worker who deserved success, and that wouldn't come if he spent his time on work he wasn't paid to do.

The sound of a saw reached her even before she opened the shop door. A motorized saw, as it turned out. Daniel had apparently found it worthwhile to install a generator for his business, much as dairy farmers like Sam and Daniel's brother had to do for their milking equipment.

She stopped inside the door, trying to find the right words while she waited. Daniel must have seen the movement when she entered, but he finished what he was cutting before he stopped the saw and stood, pulling off the safety goggles he wore.

"Rebecca. I didn't think I'd see you over here." His voice didn't express anything—not anger, not apology, nothing.

Unable to find the right words, she looked around the shop. "This is a fine setup you have here. Daad says that you've been doing a lot of remodeling jobs. It looks as if you could handle most anything with all this equipment."

"I don't think you came here to admire my shop, Rebecca."

He wasn't going to make it easier for her, in other words. Rebellion flared. He was the one who'd equated their friendship with letting him work without pay, after all.

Unfortunately, she also knew full well that if she hadn't been totally caught up in her problems, she could have handled it better, without the need for this breach between them.

She sucked in a deep breath, knowing what she had to say. "I came to tell you I'm sorry. Getting that news was a blow, but I had no right to take it out on you. Please forgive me."

His eyes were very dark in the muted light of the shop, and she couldn't tell what he was thinking. If she'd broken their friendship entirely… Panic flashed like lightning, showing her what that would mean.

"I'll forgive you on one condition." Now his smile was back, and her heart lifted. "You let me keep working on the shop."

"Maybe I didn't explain it very well." She struggled to hold on to her emotions. "When I came back, I made a promise to myself that I wouldn't lean on anyone else." The way she'd leaned on James. "I would stand on my own two feet."

"Nothing wrong with that," he said, "except that it's not the Amish way. We help one another, as you know very well. You wouldn't hesitate to help me if I needed it. Like Sam, over here every day to help do our milking, as well as his own, when Caleb was laid up. That's what we do."

Her arguments were being cut from under her, and she struggled to find a solution they both could accept.

Daniel crossed the distance between them and stood, smiling at her. "What's wrong? Can't find anything else to say?" His voice teased her gently.

"Nothing that wouldn't necessitate another apology," she said tartly. "Suppose we do this. You let me help. Surely there are things I can do. And you don't turn down other jobs to work for me."

"Deal," Daniel said. He grinned at her. "See, that wasn't so hard, was it?"

She'd tell him it was, but he wouldn't understand. None of them would, because they didn't know what her life had been like with James.

It hadn't been his fault, she told herself once again. *The injury was to blame.*

Whether that was true or not, she had to walk away from the past. She had to accept Daniel's help to do so. He held the door open to her new life, but she had to pass through, and she would.

Chapter Four

By Saturday, Daniel had begun to feel confident that Rebecca wasn't going to back out of their agreement. She showed up every day, determined to help, sometimes with Lige, sometimes by herself.

He had to admit, the work went more quickly with another pair of hands, even unskilled ones. He took a step back, assessing the shelf he'd just installed on the back wall. Rebecca wouldn't come today, he felt sure, since the Fisher family was hosting worship the next day. Everyone would be busy cleaning and cooking to prepare for the church's once-a-year visit.

So it was with considerable surprise that he heard the back door open and the now-familiar sound of Rebecca's footsteps. He lifted his eyebrows in a question when she appeared in the doorway.

"I thought you'd be completely occupied with getting ready for worship. Don't tell me your mamm let you out of the kitchen."

Her smile came more easily now than it had at first. "I tried to help, but what with Mamm and Leah and the girls, we were starting to get in each other's way. Mamm thought I'd be more use here."

"What about my little helper?" He picked up the next shelf, and she hurried to grasp the end of it.

"Lige went off with Daad and Jacob to pick up some extra peanut butter for the sandwich spread. You know my mother—she never thinks there's going to be enough food."

He nodded. It was a common enough description of most Amish mothers. "Gut that Lige is getting to know his cousin Jacob. Having a cousin just a little older will ease the path for him, especially when he starts school in the fall."

"Yah." Rebecca paused, and he suspected she was comparing steady, calm Jacob with her small son, always so shy and fearful. Then she brightened, as if she'd shoved the unwelcome thoughts away. "Lige needs to have friends to count on, like Sam and I counted on you and Caleb."

"Counted on us to keep you out of mischief, that's for sure." Keeping the talk on happy subjects was best, he thought.

"I remember it the other way around." She glanced up at him, her eyes alight, and she looked suddenly years younger. "Caleb was usually the instigator, but I remember one time when you dared Sam to jump from the hayloft. Remember? He landed right on the bags of fertilizer and broke them open. He was covered with the stuff."

He grinned. "Mostly, I remember how Sam looked, and when you started sloshing water over him, that made the mess even worse."

"And your Onkel Zeb walked in on us. He just

stood there, looking at us until you felt guilty enough to confess."

"That's Onkel Zeb, all right. I've never figured out how he does it." Daniel's smile lingered as he thought of all the times his uncle's solemn look was sufficient to get the truth.

"He put us all to work cleaning up the mess, and I didn't have anything to do with it." She gave him a playful swat and he ducked, laughing.

Laughing…and then the laughter was arrested suddenly, by his awareness of her. Rebecca, so close to him, wasn't any longer just his friend and playmate. She was a woman who seemed to draw him closer with just her smile.

Daniel drew in a shaky breath and hoped his expression hadn't changed. Ach, that wasn't right. He shouldn't be looking at Rebecca that way, or feeling the longing to find out if her lips were really as soft as they looked.

Fortunately, Rebecca didn't seem to have noticed anything, maybe because her thoughts had turned back to her son. He could read it so clearly in her expression.

"Sometimes I wish…" She let that trail off, shaking her head.

"What do you wish, Rebecca?" He kept his voice calm, interested, just the voice of a friend.

"I guess I'd like to see Lige get into a little mischief once in a while. It's natural enough for a boy that age."

He wasn't sure what to say. There were too many things he didn't understand. "It's natural enough that he's still grieving his daadi. He was probably fine before that shock, ain't so?"

For a moment, he thought she wasn't going to respond, but then she shook her head. "James had an earlier serious accident, nearly two years before he passed. I'm afraid Lige doesn't remember much of his daadi from before that."

"I didn't realize." Maybe this was what Onkel Zeb had meant when he'd spoken of the hardships she'd gone through. His heart swelled with sympathy. "I'm sorry for your trouble."

"It's…"

Her words were cut off by the front door banging open. Barry Carter, the electrician Daniel sometimes worked with, made his usual noisy entrance. "Hey, there you are!" he shouted.

Any reply vanished from Daniel's mind when he saw Rebecca's face—saw her flinch, saw her eyes fill with panic for just a brief instant before she regained control.

His wits started working again, and he stepped in front of Rebecca, screening her from view. "Barry, it's gut to see you, but do you have to come in like a tornado? You made me forget what I was measuring." His only thought was to keep talking until Rebecca had a chance to collect herself. "You got my message, yah?"

"Yep, finally listened to my answering machine. I've been that busy this spring—you wouldn't believe. You looking to move in here?" He was looking around as he spoke. Big and burly, with hands like a couple of hams, Barry had a heart as soft as butter, Daniel knew. He'd be horrified to think he'd frightened Rebecca.

Frightened. But why?

He pushed the question aside. He'd have to consider that later. "It's going to be a quilt shop for our neighbor, Rebecca Mast." A quick glance told him that Rebecca looked as if nothing ever disturbed her. "Rebecca, this is Barry Carter. He's the man to take out the electrics for you."

Recognizing the meaning of her warning glance, he added quickly, "It'll take him some time to fit you in, but this way he can check out what needs done."

"Nice to meet you, Mrs. Mast." Barry touched the bill of his ball cap in greeting. "I ought to be able to get to it by the end of the month, if there's no hurry."

"No, none at all." Rebecca sounded perfectly calm and in control. "I'm sure Daniel can show you what needs done better than I can."

Daniel nodded. "Come through to the kitchen. That's the main thing."

He led the way, with Barry following, and started explaining what needed to be done. Barry had converted Englisch houses to Amish ones before, so it didn't take all that much explaining on his part.

Which was good, because his thoughts were in a crazy jumble. Rebecca's reaction, Lige's timid behavior… He could think of one obvious reason for that, and he found his hands curling into fists at the thought.

Horrified, he forced them to relax. James Mast was dead now, and whatever his faults, he'd face a more competent judge of his life than Daniel King.

A passage came into his mind and clung there. It looked to him as if the wrong men did, as well as the good, live on after them.

Rebecca dunked her mop into the pail of sudsy water. Cleaning the cellar floor in preparation for worship tomorrow was just the sort of hard work she needed to keep her mind off what had happened.

She'd given herself away to Daniel. She'd never intended it, but the man bursting in had taken her completely by surprise. Pretending Daniel hadn't noticed was useless. He'd shielded her, stepping between her and the man and engaging him in conversation to give her time to recover.

Keeping the truth about her marriage private was becoming increasingly difficult. And Daniel seemed to know her too well.

Impulsively, she turned to Leah, working alongside her, with a question.

"Do you think we can know everything about another person if we've been close enough?"

Leah seemed to take the query seriously, as if they'd been talking about that very thing. "I guess it depends on exactly the kind of thing you're talking about. I mean, I'd say I know how Sam will react in every situation, but sometimes he proves me wrong."

She smiled, halting the rhythmic movement of the mop. "I remember one time he had an offer from a different dairy to buy our milk at a much better price. We'd been a bit short after putting in the new milk tank, and I thought he'd jump at the offer."

"He didn't?" Milk tanks and dairies didn't seem the point, but since she'd asked the question, she'd best show an interest in the answer.

"He turned them down flat. When I asked him why, he said he'd heard talk the man was trying to undercut the other dairy and had even spread rumors about the quality of their milk. Well, when I heard that, I understood. See, I might not have known that he'd turn it down, but I do know that Sam would never be associated with anyone who wasn't straight about their business. So I guess I did know him, after all."

"I'd say so." Rebecca smiled. "And that's Sam, all right. His honesty is a part of him."

"Yah, that's what I meant. If you know somebody well, you know what they're like right at the core. Who they are inside doesn't change." She shot a bright glance at Rebecca. "Even if we haven't seen them in a long time."

"I didn't..." She started to protest, and then she had to laugh at Leah's expression. "All right, I did mean Daniel."

"That's what I figured." Leah's voice was demure, but her eyes were full of mischief. "He hasn't changed all that much, ain't so?"

"That's what wonders me. He looks so different that, at first, I wasn't sure. But the more I'm around him, the more I see flashes of the boy he was. When we talk about different things that happened, it's as if no time at all has gone by."

Leah leaned on her mop, prepared to talk. "So, what was he like as a boy? I didn't know him all that well, you know."

Rebecca considered, trying to isolate the qualities Daniel had shown even as a boy. "He was steady, you know? Always calm, not easily excited. Your little Jacob reminds me of him in a way."

She nodded. "A man of few words, that's our Jacob. He's a gut peacemaker."

"Yah, exactly. That's what Daniel was, too. And..." She sought the word. "Steadfast, I guess. You could count on him to stick by you."

"Sounds to me as if Daniel isn't much different as an adult than he was as a boy, then. A gut person to have as your friend."

Leah's eyes were twinkling again, and Rebecca knew she had to protest.

"A friend, that's all. I don't want any other kind of relationship."

"You feel that now, with your husband so recently gone. But maybe, in a time, it will be different." Leah clasped her hand warmly. "You'll see. No one thought Caleb could love again after he lost his wife, but now he's happy as can be with Jessie."

"It's different for me. I...just know that marriage is not for me." Leah didn't know, couldn't know, all the reasons why it was impossible.

Leah shrugged, turning back to her mopping. "Seems to me that's Daniel's attitude, too. He acts like he's sworn off marriage. So maybe the two of you make a gut pair."

Leah didn't understand. She couldn't. But if it was true that Daniel didn't intend ever to marry, in a way, that made things easier for her. Their friendship would be less of a risk that way, and she wouldn't have to worry about either of them being hurt.

It was the first worship Sunday since she'd returned, and Rebecca was filled with happiness. Being part of worship with those who had known her since childhood made her feel that she was really home. It was a joyful step in her new life.

The usual greetings and chatter were still going on when they lined up to go in—women on one side, men on the other. Rebecca took her place in the group of young married women with Leah. Small girls were joining their mothers, while the boys joined the line of men.

Lige, though, was clinging to her skirt. She detached his hands gently. "It's time for you to go in with Grossdaadi. Remember, we talked about it."

She'd tried to rehearse everything that would happen today to make Lige feel at ease…not that it was very different from worship out in Ohio. But no matter how prepared he was, Lige seemed to be intimidated by the large group of people, all of whom knew each other.

"Komm, now." She clasped his hand to keep him from grabbing onto her again. "Do you want me to walk over with you?"

"Ach, Lige doesn't need that." Daniel squatted down beside Lige and held out his hand. "What about it? We'll go find your grossdaadi, yah?"

Lige hesitated. Then the slightest smile crossed his face, and he put his small hand into Daniel's large one. They walked off together, and Rebecca found her throat was tight.

"I never saw a bachelor so gut with the kinder as Daniel is." The woman ahead of her smiled, turning to face her. "I'm Jessie, Caleb's wife. I've been wanting to meet you, but I thought you might be too busy getting settled to want to bother with company."

"We're never too busy for you, Jessie," Leah said. "You'll come and have coffee one day this week, ain't so?"

"Do, please," Rebecca added. She'd been wanting to meet the woman Caleb had so suddenly married. It didn't take more than a glance to persuade her that they were happy. Jessie's face glowed, and Caleb's little girl pressed close against her.

"I'd like that." Jessie touched the little girl's cheek. "Becky, this is our new neighbor. She has the same name as you. Rebecca."

The child gave her a friendly stare. "Does anyone ever call you Becky?"

"No, I've always been Rebecca. A gut thing, ain't so? Or they might be mixing us up."

Becky grinned at the idea, and Rebecca smiled back.

The smile lingered on her face when she looked up, but in an instant, it vanished. One of the older women was staring at her. Lydia Schultz, it was. Rebecca remembered her, but she couldn't imagine why she was staring… It was almost as if she wanted to say something to her.

The line started moving just then, so there was no opportunity. She'd make a point of greeting Lydia afterward, she told herself.

From the moment the song leader sang the first notes of the hymn, Rebecca was giving herself up to the joy and beauty of worshipping together, hearing much-loved voices raised in praise.

When he began to speak, Bishop Thomas Braun seemed to be talking directly to her. The Scripture was the story of the Good Shepherd. Bishop Thomas spoke lovingly of Jesus carrying the lost sheep home on his shoulders, and she felt tears sting her eyes. There had been so many times in the past few years when she'd felt lost and alone. And yet she always had the sense that God was there, holding her up.

It wasn't until one of the other ministers rose

to speak that she sent a cautious glance across the room. Lige was leaning against Daadi, with his grandfather's arm around him protectively. Someone else was watching Lige, she realized. Daniel, a few benches away, let his gaze rest on her son.

Daniel's expression caught at her heart. It almost seemed he was looking at something he longed for but could never have.

The service moved on, carrying her with it, reassuring her with the familiarity of long usage. When it ended she sat still for another moment, holding on to the peace.

But there were things to be done, and she should be helping. She rose and headed for the kitchen.

In all the flurry of getting the meal on after the service ended, Rebecca didn't have time to talk with anyone except to exchange a few hurried words with Leah. She noted with amusement that even Leah's usual calm had deserted her at that point.

Lunch after worship was basically the same each time, and of course no one would admit to taking pride in how well they did it. But that didn't stop every woman from wanting lunch to go perfectly when she was in charge. Leah had everyone scurrying to follow orders, and Rebecca caught more than one longsuffering expression from her kinder.

Finally everyone had been fed, and the kitchen crew could sit down at the tables to finish. Since the weather had turned warm, the tables had been set up outside, and it was pleasant to relax and enjoy the scene.

Some of the older girls had organized a baseball game with a plastic bat and ball for the younger children, while the babies had been rounded up on blankets in the care of older siblings and cousins. Rebecca scanned the group for Lige, spotting him at last on the fringe of the game. He wasn't alone—Daniel was with him. He was patiently showing her son how to swing at the ball.

Rebecca started toward them, torn between her desire not to bother Daniel and her delight in her son's obvious happiness. She was still a few paces away when Lige finally connected with the ball. He was so startled he dropped the bat. Then a huge grin split his face.

"Gut job," Daniel said. "I think you're ready to play with the others. Just remember to keep looking at the ball, whether you're catching or hitting it."

"I will. Denke, Daniel." Lige hesitated, and for an instant she thought he was going to hug Daniel. He stopped short of that, and Daniel, maybe understanding more than she'd thought, patted him lightly on the shoulder.

When Lige had run off to join the other children, Rebecca approached Daniel. "Denke, from me, too, Daniel. That was wonderful kind of you."

"Ach, it was my pleasure. He's a gut lad, that boy of yours." He hesitated, and she could see a question in his eyes. "I wondered… Well, Lige said that his daadi didn't ever play ball with him."

"No." The sadness gripped her for what might have been. "James was never himself again after that first accident. I don't think Lige even remembers him from before that."

"James had brothers, yah? A father?"

She nodded. It was so hard to explain what it had

been like to someone who hadn't lived through it. "His daad tried, but it seemed to upset James to see someone else interfering. People just started leaving us alone rather than upset him."

"I'm sorry. It sounds like it was hard on everyone."

"That's so." Rebecca was relieved to have brushed through the subject without more difficulty. "I'd best go and let Leah put me to work again." She walked away quickly.

Leah was cleaning one of the tables, so Rebecca joined her, filling up a tray with as much as she could carry. As they walked together toward the kitchen with their loads, Leah scanned the group scattered around the yard.

"Don't tell me you're trying to press your kinder into service again," Rebecca said, a laugh in her voice.

"Just making sure they're not skimping on the work." Leah glanced at her and smiled. "I know, I know, they all think I fuss too much when we have worship here."

"Wait until they have homes of their own. Then they'll understand. We were probably the same way."

"I suppose so, but don't let my kinder hear you say that." Leah stepped cautiously up onto the porch, wary of the heavy tray. "You're happy, ain't so?"

"Yah, I guess I am. Seems as if being back in worship with everyone was gut for me." She frowned, wanting to explain and not sure she could. "Not that I didn't love worship in Ohio. But with everyone knowing about James's injury and…well, everything else. I felt like people were either feeling sorry for me or blaming me."

"Blaming you?" Leah's eyebrows rose. "Surely no

one would think it was your fault that James was the way he was."

Rebecca shrugged, trying to hold the screen door with her elbow. "You can never tell what folks will think. Anyway, I'm just as glad to leave it behind."

They stepped inside. Only a few women were left in the kitchen, but they weren't cleaning up. Instead, they were gathered around Lydia Schultz. At the sight of Rebecca, several of the women averted their eyes and abruptly became busy. Lydia didn't. She stared at Rebecca, as she'd done in worship, while a flood of color swept over her face.

Rebecca stood where she was, clutching the tray, unable for the moment to move. She knew only too well what that reaction meant. They had been talking about her.

It seemed she wasn't able to leave the past behind, even here.

Chapter Five

Daniel got to the house earlier than usual on Monday, intent on unloading his wagon before Rebecca showed up. If she realized he'd brought some extra materials, she'd be intent on either paying for them or stopping work if she couldn't. So the best thing was not to tell her, it seemed to him.

Picking up several planks, he headed in through the back door, stepping over the broken board automatically. He'd got inside the kitchen when he realized he hadn't had to use the key Rebecca had given him. At almost the same moment, a footstep from the shop area froze him in his tracks.

The door to the shop swung open, and Daniel relaxed. Not Rebecca, thank the gut Lord.

He grinned at Sam. "It's just you, Sam."

Sam's eyebrows lifted. "What do you mean, just me? Who were you worried about?"

"Rebecca." He moved past Sam to deposit the planks on the stack of them against the wall.

Sam planted himself between Daniel and the door.

"Komm on, spill it. Why don't you want to see Rebecca?"

"I do want to," he protested. "I don't want her to see me with this load of supplies, or she'll try to either pay me for them or insist on stopping work if she can't."

"So you thought you'd go around her." Sam's expression was disapproving for an instant, and then he grinned. "What are you waiting for? Let's get the rest of it in."

Together they carried the remaining supplies in. Sam took a step back and assessed the stack of planks and the box of brackets. "Aren't you afraid she'll notice it's different?"

Daniel considered. "I don't think so." He shoved the box under a tarp with his foot. "Would Leah?"

"Probably not. Now, if it was a question of something she worked with, she'd be on it in a second, but not this." He frowned for a moment, sketching a movement as if to pull out money. "Let me take care of this."

"Forget it."

"I ought to cover it," Sam protested. "She's my sister, not yours."

"She's my friend, and it's my job. Now, forget about it. I warn you, I'm going to lose my temper if you persist."

"Hah! You never do. At least, not since you were about ten. Then I seem to recall a certain episode where I ended up in the pond because I was teasing your little brother."

"I didn't really push you," Daniel said, remembering that hot August day. "We were all looking for an excuse to get wet anyhow."

"Not pushed, maybe. You just managed to stick

your big foot out, so when Caleb jostled me, I tripped and landed in the pond."

"At least we all joined you." The water had felt so good after a couple of hours spent working in the sun.

"Yah." Sam grinned. "I could probably be stricter with my own kinder if I didn't have such a memory of doing the same things when I was their age."

"I'd best unhitch Molly before I start to work." Daniel headed back outside, Sam following. They worked together to unhitch the placid buggy horse, and Sam led her into the fenced-in paddock behind the house.

"So, what are you going to tell Rebecca when she sees you brought a horse and wagon with you this time?" Sam asked.

"That I had planned a stop in town today, before I came. That's true enough, and she won't ask what I went for." He'd thought it out, knowing he couldn't give Rebecca the slightest hint that he'd paid for those supplies, unless he wanted an argument.

He and Sam stood, watching the mare for a moment, arms resting on the fence rail. Sam had something more to say. Daniel could read his face too well not to know that. So he waited.

Finally Sam shook his head. "I wish I knew what was going on with Rebecca. She's my kid sister. Wouldn't you think she'd confide in me? We all know…" He seemed to change his mind about the direction that sentence was going. "We all want to help her, but she keeps shutting us out. Makes me want to shake her."

He'd have to be careful about this, Daniel decided. He didn't know everything, but he did have a little insight into why Rebecca was so determined to stand on her own.

"I don't think shaking is a gut idea," he said.

"No. But I have to do something." Sam pounded his fist against the railing in a sudden gesture. "If she were your little sister, you'd want to help her. You'd do anything..."

His words cut short, and embarrassment flooded his face. "Sorry, Dan. I didn't mean to make you think about Aaron."

"I know." The ache that always lurked in his heart made itself felt. "If I knew where Aaron was, I'd do anything to bring him home safe again, but I don't."

"Yah, I know." Sam buffeted his shoulder awkwardly. "We all pray for him."

Daniel could only nod. He swallowed the lump in his throat and forced himself to concentrate on Rebecca. "Maybe the best thing for Rebecca is to let her tell you what's going on when she's ready."

"That's what Leah says," Sam admitted. "I want a little more action."

He could understand. That fierce need to do something...anything...to help the one you felt responsible for—that was what he felt constantly. But that didn't mean it was the best choice.

"Leah's a wise woman." It was all he could think to say. "Rebecca seems like she's been through a lot. Maybe she just needs time."

"If only she'd let us give her the money she needs." Sam's steady gaze focused on his face. "You know I'd give you the money for this job in a minute."

"Not unless you want to end up in the pond again."

"I'd like to see you try." The concern in Sam's face dissolved in a smile.

Daniel turned back toward the house. "Well, this isn't getting any work done. I figure that's all I can do for Rebecca right now—get her shop ready to open. She'll maybe start feeling better about herself once she knows she has money coming in."

"I guess you're right. Suppose I give you a hand until she comes and kicks me out. Okay?"

Daniel nodded. He understood Sam's frustration, because he felt it himself. But nobody was going to be able to take care of Rebecca until she decided to let them, and he didn't know if that would be ever.

Rebecca straightened her back and stretched when she and Daniel finished attaching the counter to the floor.

"I never realized how hard carpenters work. I'll be more grateful in the future."

Grinning, Daniel rose easily to his feet. He seemed able to work steadily no matter how difficult the circumstance. "It's really coming along, isn't it?"

Rebecca's breath caught as she looked around the room—her shop. It shouldn't come as a surprise to her, since she'd helped with just about every inch of it, but still, the change from an empty room into an actual shop astonished her. Had it really come about so quickly?

"I'm wonderful glad. And thankful." She glanced at him to be sure he knew it was him she was thanking, as well as the gut Lord. "I can actually start planning where to put things. How long, do you think, until I can clean and start arranging stock?"

Daniel seemed to be counting up the time to accomplish what was left. "Not long. Maybe by tomorrow afternoon, we can get on to the cleaning."

"We?" She shook her head. "That's not part of your job."

"Now that's where you're wrong," Daniel said. "I always do a thorough cleanup when I finish a job. I tell my customers that, when I leave, it'll be ready for them to use. And I mean it." He smiled at her expression. "Don't start arguing with me, now. It's part of my satisfaction in a job well-done."

It was hard to argue with that, and she suspected that was why he'd said it. He went on quickly, before she could pursue the subject.

"Do you have enough to put everything on display? And what about the racks? Is anything else needed?"

Rebecca tabulated display areas. "I think this is all that's needed. I was thinking that a cradle would be nice to show off the baby quilts, but I can find one somewhere, I'm sure. And I won't have enough fabric bolts to begin with, but once I have money coming in, I'll be able to order more."

She could almost feel the sympathy in his look. "Nothing from your brother-in-law yet?"

"I'm sure it will come any day now." Rebecca hoped she sounded more optimistic than she felt. "As for the number of quilts, I was worried at first, but Leah has brought in several that people want to sell on consignment."

"That's great, ain't so? So why do you look concerned about it?"

How could he tell? That was the problem in dealing with a childhood friend. They knew you too well.

"I'm not concerned about the stock. It's just that ever since Leah got the idea of bringing things in on consignment, she's been working on that like crazy. I don't want…"

"What?" Daniel gave her an exasperated look. "To accept her help? Knowing Leah, I'd guess she's having the time of her life."

She had to smile. "You know, she is. I wish I had half her energy and determination. But she has her own work to do, and I shouldn't monopolize her time."

"If that's all that's worrying you, I'd say to forget it. As far as I can tell, it's giving her a lot of fun. Probably she enjoys the idea of being a part of your business."

"But…"

"And if it's the fact that she's doing something for you, why don't you offer her part of the commission on the sales she brings in?"

Daniel seemed content to let that sink in, leaning against the counter, studying her face.

Amusement bubbled in her. "You're looking very self-satisfied," she said. "You think you have me figured out."

"Don't I?" The twinkle in his eyes became evident. "You haven't changed all that much over the years. And I think Leah would be pleased to have something other than the kinder to spend her energy on."

"I hadn't thought of it that way," she admitted, turning the idea over in her mind. It was very tempting to consider sharing even a portion of the burden with someone else. "Maybe I'll mention it to her."

"You'll soon have your chance," he said, looking past her out the front window. "Looks as if Leah has been to the mailbox and is stopping here."

Rebecca turned and watched her sister-in-law approach. Was it too much to hope that, in her bundle of mail, there was a check from John?

The door swung open. Leah stopped just inside, looking around. "My goodness, just look at this place. How much you've got done in the last few days! You'll be ready to open soon, ain't so?"

"I guess so." Rebecca's stomach fluttered at the thought. "I suppose there's a lot I should do to get the word out to folks."

"Yah, signs up on bulletin boards all over town, a big sign out front... Ach, Rebecca, I almost envy you. I've always thought I'd be good at running a business, but I've been so busy with the family, I haven't had time to think about it. Anyway, what could I do?"

Daniel evidently took that as a signal, because he nudged her.

She ignored him. What if she asked and Leah only agreed out of pity for her? If she...

"Funny thing," Daniel said, "we were just talking about you." Ignoring her glare, he went on. "Rebecca wondered if you'd be interested in taking on the consignment side of things. For a share of the profit, of course."

"Only if..." Rebecca began, and then she stopped. The answer was written all over Leah's face. It lit up like the sun coming out on a cloudy day.

"You mean it?" She acted as if they'd offered her a wonderful gift. "I'd love to. You wouldn't have to give me anything..."

"I couldn't do that," Rebecca said quickly. "It wouldn't be right. Our arrangement would have to be business. A percentage of the sales. What do you think?"

"Ach, you can tell, can't you?" Leah seized her hands and squeezed them. "It would make me wonderful happy to be a part of the shop." Dropping her hands, Leah moved a few steps away, seeming to picture the place filled with quilts and quilting supplies. "I have so many ideas. I can't wait to get started. I must make a list of all the people I want to contact."

Daniel spoke in Rebecca's ear. "I hope we haven't unleashed something you can't control."

A gurgle of laughter welled up in her as she turned to face him. "I'm glad there's not a creek nearby. You're so ready to push that you'd probably push me into that as well, the way you did Sam."

"Only if I knew you really wanted to go in," he said, his face solemn but his eyes dancing.

Rebecca started to say something tart about his habit of thinking he knew best. But her gaze met his laughing eyes, and the words got all tangled up in her head. Her breath caught, and her heart seemed to swell. Heat rushed to her face, shocking her.

She ought to look away. She ought to say something light to hide the feelings.

But emotions were bubbling inside of her and flooding her senses. She wanted…

Reality hit with a crash. She could not be feeling this… She didn't want to give it a name. She couldn't very well deny it. But even so, she couldn't have felt anything for Daniel except friendship. That was all. Friendship.

Daniel moved a couple of careful steps away from Rebecca, reading only too clearly the play of emotions on her face and knowing they were echoed on his own. Where had that flare of man-and-woman attraction come from? If he'd felt it earlier for Rebecca, he'd denied it, but he couldn't deny this, not when both of them felt it.

It was impossible. That was what he kept telling himself. He couldn't risk marrying and then letting down someone he loved again. And yet…Caleb must have felt some of the same guilt he had, and Caleb had moved on, finding happiness with Jessie. Was it too much to think it could happen for him?

Rebecca seemed to have conquered whatever she'd felt very quickly. She and Leah were chattering away a mile a minute about the shop, and he could watch her without her noticing.

Leah was good for her—he could see it. Leah had such a positive, upbeat attitude that it was infectious. Rebecca had been like that once, too. He had a fairly good idea what had changed her, but she persisted in trying to hide it.

Maybe, if she wouldn't confide in him, she'd confide in Leah. Perhaps she'd feel more comfortable talking to another woman, and Leah was safe. He knew instinctively Rebecca wouldn't burden her mother with the knowledge, knowing what pain it would cause.

Both of them turned in his direction, and he tried to look as if he were intent on his work. Fortunately they weren't, as it turned out, paying attention to him.

"I'd best get back to the house and see how much mess Mary Ann has created making snickerdoodles with the little ones." Leah's smile denied any expectation she had of finding a mess. Mary Ann, her eldest daughter, seemed to love nothing better than tending the little ones.

"Isn't she in school today? Or did you keep her home just to bake cookies?" he teased.

"Her cold seemed a bit worse this morning, so I thought she'd best stay in. But she seems to be getting her pep back now."

"We should relieve her," Rebecca said. "I can imagine what Lige and your little Miriam are doing with the cookie dough." She was smiling and acting normally now, as if she'd forgotten any emotional upset already.

"I'll handle it," Leah said, scooting out the door. "You get on with your work. Your daad wants to have Lige do some planting with him, so he'll be well occupied."

Rebecca nodded and let her go, and he thought she showed a little constraint when she turned back to him. "It'll be sehr gut for Lige to work alongside his grossdaadi, so they can get to know each other better."

"They haven't had much time together." He asked the question that wondered him, "Why didn't you visit more often when you were out in Ohio?"

Rebecca seemed to draw into herself. "James couldn't get away from the farm."

He guessed she wanted him to accept that, but he felt compelled to push a bit harder. Surely a friend had that right.

"You and Lige could have visited without him," he pointed out.

For an instant, he thought she'd snap at him, but she

didn't. "James didn't like to be left alone." She turned away, signaling that the conversation was over.

She was hugging her pain to herself, and that hurt him.

"Ach, Rebecca, you can trust me with the whole story. Don't you know that?"

Rebecca looked up, startled at his tone, her eyes wide, her face softening. If she would only speak...

The sound of someone on the porch had her retreating. Frustrated, he frowned at the door, wishing the intruder well away from them.

The door opened, and he was surprised to see Eli Gaus coming in. Eli, a couple of years younger than him, was partners in the sawmill with his father and brother.

"Eli." He tried to sound welcoming. "If you're here to try and sell me another batch of two-by-fours, I have plenty."

Eli's serious expression sat oddly on his youthful, freckled face. "Your brother said you were working over here, so I figured I'd drop by." He seemed ill at ease, and he glanced at Rebecca. "Could I have a word? In private, I mean." He gave Rebecca an apologetic smile.

"Of course. I'll be measuring the back windows for shades if you want me," she said.

Daniel waited until she'd gone and then looked at Eli, frowning a little. "What's happening?"

If anything, Eli's awkwardness increased. "I... Well, the thing is, it's about your brother. About Aaron."

The name hit him like a blow. People so seldom mentioned Aaron, who had jumped the fence years ago, that it was odd to hear it. Not that he ever stopped thinking of him or stopped wondering.

"What about Aaron? Not...not bad news?"

"Ach, no, not exactly. Sorry." Eli's fair skin reddened. "I didn't mean you to think that. You see, I saw him."

"You saw him?" He repeated the words, only half believing. It had been so long since they'd had any word at all. "Where?"

"I was out in Indiana for a wedding." Now that he'd got started, Eli seemed to find it easier. "One of the cousins took me for a ride past the racetrack where they sometimes get buggy horses. Aaron was working there."

"How is he? Did you speak to him?" *Did he say anything about us?* That was really what he wanted to ask.

"He looked all right, I guess. Seemed funny to see him there, but he always was one for the horses, ain't so?"

Daniel managed a smile, thinking of a small Aaron walking right up to a mammoth Percheron and lifting its hoof to remove a stone. "Yah, he was. So he's working with the horses there at the racetrack?"

"He's a trainer, he said." Eli hesitated. "The other guys around were a pretty rough bunch, I thought. Not like the horse people we're used to."

He understood, he guessed. Most Amish in farm country had a relationship with the Englisch horse people around, building barns, serving as farriers to Englisch and Amish alike, going to the same livestock auctions.

"Did he seem happy?" He couldn't make his brother

come back and be one of them, but he still wished him happiness.

Eli considered the question. "He seemed like he fitted in with them, I guess. But happy? I don't know. One thing, though. You can't let him know I told you. I agreed I wouldn't, but when my Elizabeth heard about it, she scolded me up one side and down the other. Said his family at least had the right to know he's alive."

He was looking at Daniel pleadingly, obviously caught between loyalty to his childhood friend and his wife's firm belief in what was right.

Daniel nodded, the fact sinking in. Aaron was alive and apparently well. But he couldn't reach out to him, and no matter how he looked at it, he'd still failed his little brother.

It was a lesson to him. He'd begun to think he might let Rebecca depend on him, but he couldn't. He didn't dare.

Chapter Six

Rebecca knelt at the overgrown flower bed along the side of the house, cleaning away the dead leaves that had blown there over the winter. How much was left of the colorful plantings she remembered, the ones old Mrs. Evans had tended so lovingly?

She'd heard Daniel's visitor leave a good half hour ago, but Daniel hadn't called to her to come and help him, so she'd left him alone. There had been something in his face when he'd walked out to the porch with Eli that had warned her off. She didn't know what they'd been talking about, but it must have been something serious.

Eli Gaus had been younger than they were, but she remembered him as a freckle-faced child, inclined to mischief. He'd been a good friend of Aaron's, as she recalled. All grown-up now, like all of those children she'd once shared a schoolroom with.

Yes, his visit had had something to do with Daniel's brother Aaron—she'd caught the name before the door closed and she'd moved away. She'd been married before Aaron jumped the fence, but Mamm had passed on the news in her weekly letter. It had hit his family hard, Mamm had said, as was natural. Daniel had always looked after his little brother, so he'd have had trouble coming to terms with it.

If Eli had come to discuss something about Aaron... well, she wouldn't pry. If Daniel wanted to confide in her, he would.

Brushing aside the last of the leaves, Rebecca found the fresh green spears of tulips. Her heart lifted at the sight. The clump of daffodils at the corner was already blooming, and they'd look much better once everything was cleared around them. Nothing said spring quite as well as tulips and daffodils.

If only she could have the flower beds looking their best before her opening...but she could only do what she had time for. It was more important to have some money coming in right now than to make things perfect.

"Finding some treasures?" Daniel had come up behind her so softly she hadn't heard him on the fresh grass.

She looked up at him and shielded her eyes. With the sun behind him, he looked enormous. Brushing dirt from her hands, she rose to her feet.

"Mrs. Evans had flowers all along this side of the house. I'd like to see it looking that way again."

"It's been neglected for a time, but it'll come back." He squatted to clear some dead branches away from a small shrub. "This is a miniature lilac." He cradled a tiny bud in his hand. "It'll bloom this year. Just needs a little loving care." Now he looked up at her. "About what happened before, when Eli came... I'm sorry for asking you to go out of your own place."

"That's all right." She spoke quickly, trying to hide

her desire to know what had set that frown in his eyes. She'd seen it there from the moment he came out. Eli had left him with a problem for sure. She longed to know what it was.

"I…I heard him say it was something about Aaron. I hope he's all right."

"Fine." Daniel snapped out the word as he stood. "It wasn't important."

In other words, he had no intention of sharing his problem with her. She nodded, unable to think of any answer that wouldn't sound like prying.

"Maybe we should get back to work." She started to move toward the door, but he stopped her with a gesture.

"Sorry." He seemed to be fighting a battle within himself, but finally he gave a rueful smile. "I'm not practicing what I preach, am I? I wanted you to talk to me about your troubles, but I slam the door in your face when you expect the same."

"It's not so easy, is it? Some things… They're just too hard to talk about."

He grimaced, shaking his head. "I'll have to talk about this. To tell Onkel Zeb and Caleb, anyway. Maybe I should practice on you." Daniel's chest moved as he drew in a deep breath. "Eli saw Aaron when he was out in Indiana recently. Talked to him in fact."

So that was it. He was hurting at the reminder that Aaron was out there in the Englisch world and hadn't cared enough to let his family know where he was.

"Is he well?" she asked, aware of the need to tread carefully.

"So Eli said." Daniel's voice was tight with pain. "He didn't send any word to us. Doesn't want us bothering him, I guess."

"Oh, Daniel, I'm sure it's not that." She struggled for another explanation. "Maybe he's afraid you'll make him feel bad about going away."

She'd like to have Aaron here right now. She'd give him a good shake for letting people who loved him worry this way.

"I guess I'd feel less guilty if I knew he was happy enough with his decision that he could still have a relationship with his family. You know what I mean. Lots of families have someone who jumped the fence, but they still get along all right."

She nodded, but she was fixed on the one word. *Guilty?* She knew, only too well, how responsible Daniel had felt for his little brother, especially after his mother left. So of course he felt guilty for losing him—as if he'd lost his grip on his brother's hand in the crowd at an auction.

"He's a grown man, Daniel." She kept her words gentle, not wanting him to shut her out again. "We can't keep people from following their own paths, no matter how much we love them."

Her thoughts spiraled off into the past, to James's mother turning on her after his fall, saying she should have stopped him from doing anything so dangerous. They'd both known at the time that nothing stopped James when he was determined, but maybe it made his mamm feel better to blame someone else.

Daniel didn't look convinced or comforted by her words. Naturally not. She was trying to do what she'd just said was impossible—to keep Daniel from the path of blaming himself. He wouldn't stop. He couldn't. And if he could… She faced the stark reality. If he could, he wouldn't be the man he was.

* * *

It wasn't until milking time that Daniel was able to get Caleb and Onkel Zeb alone together. Caleb would probably tell Jessie about Aaron of course, but he wouldn't want to do it in front of the children.

The usual milking routine ran along smoothly, and they could work and talk at the same time, often laughing together over the events of the day. But not this time. Not when Daniel had told them about Eli finding Aaron.

For a moment, no one spoke, and the only sound was the steady murmur of the milking machine.

"We must go after him," Caleb said, his jaw setting in the way it did when he was determined. "We must see him and persuade him to return home where he belongs."

Daniel had known that was what he'd say. "But what about Eli? You know what friends they were. He doesn't want Aaron to know that he gave him away."

"This is too important for childish promises. His wife saw that, even if Eli didn't. Eli is a grown man, and so is Aaron. It's time Aaron came home. He belongs here." Caleb was looking and sounding like the head of the family.

Daniel knew his love for his little brother was real, but he also knew that Caleb had never had much patience with Aaron. Caleb had grown out of that impatience in time, and he was a gentle and patient father to his young ones. But then... Well, neither of them had been old enough for the responsibilities thrust on them when their family fell apart.

"What if Aaron doesn't want to return?" Daniel tried to shrug away the tension that rode him. "I'd do anything to have Aaron home, but it wouldn't be much use if he didn't want to be here."

He turned to Onkel Zeb before Caleb could answer. "You haven't said anything yet, Onkel Zeb. What do you think?"

His uncle's lean, weathered face was taut, his faded blue eyes pained. His grief over their missing one had never been so obvious, and it hurt to look at. A quick glance at Caleb told him that his older brother was similarly affected.

"Yah," Caleb said, his voice husky. "What should we do?"

"Nothing," he said at last, and the word seemed to carry a heavy weight. "It would be wrong to break Eli's trust, but even if it were not so, I'd say the same."

"But Onkel Zeb…" Caleb began.

"Ach, Caleb, do you think I don't understand? But you reminded us that Aaron is a grown man now. He's not the little boy who sat on my knee."

"We can't forget him." Daniel's heart hurt. "We have to do something, but what?"

"Wait. Have patience." Onkel Zeb put a hand on his shoulder and reached out to Caleb with the other. They stood there in silence for a moment, linked. "And pray that God will show him the way home."

Rebecca's words echoed in his mind. *We can't keep people from following their own paths, no matter how much we love them.*

He wanted to argue. He was responsible for Aaron. He always had been. He was his brother's keeper.

Rebecca stood, holding the door of the shop open, marveling at what had been accomplished in a couple of days. The carpentry work was complete, and the entire place spotless. And here came a wave of people bringing the merchandise to stock the store for its opening tomorrow.

Her stomach gave a little flip at the thought. Tomorrow! After all the work and heartache, her dream was about to come true.

She stepped back, letting a line of nieces and nephews carrying boxes get past, and then hurried to show them where each should be placed. When she started to open a box, Mary Ann—Sam and Leah's oldest girl—took it from her.

"I'll see that all the fabric gets out on the tables," she said. "I know just how you want them. The young ones will help," she added, from the superiority of her twelve years.

Rebecca gave way. She'd pictured herself doing all the unpacking and arranging, but she could no more stop the flow of determined people than she could stop Lost Creek in its course. All of her family was there of course, and all of Daniel's kin as well, along with several of the women who'd brought quilts for consignment. Their happy chatter filled the air.

Leah and Jessie, Caleb's wife, were following Mamm's directions as they started hanging display items, and she hurried to help them.

"What do you think?" Leah held out her arms, a quilt draped over each. "The Sunshine and Shadows next to the Broken Star? Or should it be the Log Cabin?"

She'd made the Broken Star pattern when she was expecting Lige, and it was dear to her for that reason. But the other two seemed a better match to go side by side. "Let's put these two next to each other, and then that pretty heart applique one. I want a mix of the consignment quilts with mine, and I like the way the colors go."

"Wonderful gut," Jessie said. "The colors flow into one another. It will look like a rainbow once they're all up." She lifted one of the quilts, and the curve of her belly spoke of the new baby who'd soon arrive, not that anyone would mention it with the men and boys around.

Silly, she supposed, but that was the custom. No one would talk about the forthcoming baby in mixed company until it was safe in its crib. She gave Jessie the knowing smile that one mother would give to another. Caleb was truly blessed in his second wife—a wonderful mammi to his two kinder and now a new baby to fill their house with joy.

Mamm was unpacking a box with smaller items, like wall hangings and place mats. "I put in some of my quilted pot holders," she said. "Some folks will come tomorrow just to see what's what. They maybe won't be ready to buy a quilt, but they'll want to spend money on something, and the pot holders will be gut for them."

Rebecca felt joy bubbling up inside her. To be here, her goal within reach and her family supporting her— what more could she ask?

"You're a wise woman, Mammi." Rebecca helped her put them on the small stand Daniel had cleverly contrived. "I'm certain sure you're right about it." She paused with a pot holder made of a folded star in her hand. "This is too pretty ever to pick up a hot kettle with."

"So someone can use it to set the teapot on," Mamm said. "No reason why something can't be pretty as well as useful."

Jessie was nodding in agreement. "I heard an Englischer say a quilted piece was a work of art, and I thought that was a funny way to look at it. But maybe she was right. We don't think of it as art when we're stitching, but if it brings folks joy, what difference does it make what you call it?"

Leah chuckled. "Mostly I'm thinking it's a gut reason to sit for a time and sew something more interesting than the holes the boys make in their knees."

"Better for kinder to wear out their clothes than their sheets," Mamm said, repeating the old saying as if it were new today.

"For sure," Rebecca replied. Any mother would a hundred times rather be sick herself than have her child sick.

"Look." Leah touched her arm, nodding toward the door. "Your daad and Zeb have a surprise for you."

Rebecca swung around and froze, hardly able to believe her eyes. Daadi and Daniel's onkel Zeb stood there, holding a sign between them, both of them grinning self-consciously.

And what a sign—the lettering was so clear and neat it looked as if it had been done by a professional. It said Rebecca's Quilts, and below it was a painted representation of a quilted square, its colors bright.

"Daad, Zeb..." She rushed toward them, blinking back tears. "It's so beautiful. You made it for me?"

"I did the design and Zeb did the painting," Daadi said, beaming. "He's a wonderful gut hand with a brush, that's certain sure."

"I can't believe it." She ran her hand lightly over the painted surface. "Denke. How can I ever thank you enough?"

"Ach, it's nothing," Zeb said. "We had a gut time with it. And Daniel put in the posts and hardware, so we can hang it outside."

"Your customers have to know where to find you, ain't so?" Daad said. "You keep on with your work, and we'll get it put up."

She couldn't help watching them as they carefully carried it out to where Sam waited next to a pair of posts that seemed to have appeared when she wasn't looking. Daniel's doing, of course. Where had he got to? She had to thank him.

Glancing around at the busy figures in the shop, she saw everyone, it seemed, except Daniel. Silly to feel the loss when he wasn't there. He had other work to do, that was certain.

Joshua, her oldest nephew, maneuvered a stepladder past her and set it up beside the door. She looked at him with a question in her face.

Joshua blushed a little, showing her the object he was carrying—a small bell. "Lots of shops have a bell on the door, so I thought you should, too. That way, if you're busy in the back, you'll know when a customer comes in."

She wanted to give him an enormous hug but restrained herself. Boys his age were unaccountable, and it might embarrass him. She contented herself with a warm smile.

"That is so very thoughtful of you, Joshua. And you're right—it's just what I need. Denke."

His color deepened, and he ducked his head. "I'll

get it fastened up right away," he said and scurried up the stepladder.

Rebecca stood smiling, looking around the shop. It was taking shape beautifully. But she shouldn't stand and watch while other people were working for her. She joined Mary Ann, who was directing her young crew in arranging the bolts of fabric.

"This is the way you want it, ain't so?" Her niece looked a little anxious, eager to get it right. "All the prints together, and all the solid colors together right across from them."

"That's right." She patted Mary Ann's shoulder. "You're doing a wonderful gut job. You even got Lige and Jessie's little ones doing something useful."

"We didn't want them running around underfoot." Mary Ann was as practical as her mother. "And they really do want to help. Lige especially."

"Yah." Rebecca watched her son, pleased. "It's important that he know he's contributing his share."

Mary Ann tilted her head, as if turning that over in her mind. "I didn't think of it that way, but I see what you mean. Grossmammi says that in a family, everyone works for all."

"That's what she always taught us." The impact of her mother's oft-repeated phrase stuck in her mind. They were family, and it was important that she let them help for their sakes, not just hers. She'd lost sight of that in her need to stand on her own feet.

Mary Ann straightened a bolt, stroking the fabric. "I wondered… Well, maybe, if you like…I could help you in the store sometimes."

Rebecca bit back a quick response that she could handle it. What had she just been telling herself?

"That would be a big help, Mary Ann. After all, I'll want to take a break sometimes, and I'll need someone I can trust."

Mary Ann's wide smile was all the response she needed.

Mamm, coming up behind her, slipped her arm around Rebecca's waist. "Mary Ann is that, all right. Now, come and tell me which of the table runners you want displayed."

They were deep into a discussion on what to display where when she heard the back door open and close. Not surprising on this busy day, but everyone seemed to have fallen silent at the moment. She turned to look.

Daniel had just come in, and he carried a large maple cradle in his arms.

"The cradle. Ach, that's perfect for showing off the baby quilts," Leah said. "Isn't it perfect, Rebecca?"

"It's just exactly right." Rebecca blinked back a quick tear. Everyone was being so kind…and not just kind but thoughtful. "How did you know I wanted a cradle?" She helped Daniel put it into position.

"You mentioned it one day, and I remembered when I went to an auction, so I bid on it." He grinned. "You should have heard the men making fun of me, but I made them promise they wouldn't mention it. I wanted it to be a surprise."

"You succeeded." She stroked the curve of the maple, marveling at the condition of the cradle. "You must have refinished it to have it looking so good."

He nodded, reaching past her to show her the underside of the cradle. "The legs and the rockers just needed some work, that was the main thing. I didn't dare try to take the one that's in the attic. Caleb wouldn't let me out of the house with it."

"I can imagine."

Daniel righted the cradle, and his hand brushed hers. Rebecca tried to ignore the warm tingle that spread up her arm at his touch. His fingers moved slightly against her skin, almost as if he were stroking it the way she had stroked the cradle.

For an instant, he didn't pull away, but then he straightened, looking around the shop as if nothing had happened. "It's almost ready."

"Yah, thanks to everyone's help."

"Helping has made them happy," he said softly, just for her ears.

Her gaze tangled with his. "I know," she said. "I understand now. Doing it together is gut for all of us."

Chapter Seven

Rebecca found it impossible to eat breakfast the next morning. Her stomach was filled with so many butterflies that she couldn't possibly put any food in it. Instead, she busied herself helping Mamm and Leah in packing up the food they insisted on bringing to the shop opening.

She took a tin of snickerdoodles from her mother. "Mammi, I don't think any customers we have are expecting to be fed just because they come to the opening."

"You're just not thinking then," Mamm replied tartly. "Most likely half the church, at least, will stop by sometime today to wish you well. The least we can do is have some coffee and snacks for them."

Leah nudged her. "No point in arguing. If you have food, someone will eat it. If it's not used up, the kinder will finish it off in no time."

Mary Ann hurried into the kitchen from outside. "I have the pony cart all ready to take the coffeepots and cookies to the shop. Shall I start loading?"

"Yah, for sure." Leah handed her a basket and a large tin. "Get the young ones to help you."

Rebecca, realizing no one was paying any attention to her protests, picked up a box containing a couple of coffeepots and headed out. Clearly the decision was out of her hands. When Mamm, who was always so soft-spoken, gave instructions in that voice, they had to be obeyed, no matter how old you were.

It was pleasant to be walking up the lane with Leah in the wake of the pony cart, each of them carrying a few things there hadn't been room for. The weather had cooperated, and surely the spring warmth and sunshine would encourage people to come out.

"It's a gut day for a new venture," Leah said. "Look, there's a whole patch of lilies of the valley blooming where Mrs. Evans used to have her bench. She always said how sweet they smelled when she sat there."

"I hadn't even noticed them before Sam and Joshua cleared out some of the overgrown brush." Rebecca shook her head. "I told Sam they had enough to do, but he didn't listen."

"Sam's gut at not hearing what he doesn't want to," Leah said, her eyes twinkling.

Rebecca chuckled. "He always was, as I remember."

"We'll set up in the kitchen," Leah said, going up the porch steps. "Mary Ann will help. Then we can just carry trays into the front as we need to refill them. I was thinking to use that table in the corner of the shop for the coffee and cookies, yah?"

"That sounds fine, except that there's so much lumber stored in the kitchen…" But as they went in, she discovered that was no longer the case. Even now,

Daniel was carrying the last few things toward the living room.

"Almost done," he said. "I wiped down the counters, too."

"You didn't need..." she began.

Daniel shook his head at her. "Leah told me to. I didn't want to get on her bad side when I heard she was making whoopie pies."

Leah laughed. "Daniel is easy to manage. He responds to food like most men."

Mary Ann, leading her group of small helpers, began bringing things in and putting them on the counter, and for a few minutes, Rebecca was too busy to talk. But soon Leah was sweeping the younger ones out on the porch, promising that she'd bring them cookies in a few minutes if they stayed there.

Lige detoured on his way to the porch to tug on Rebecca's apron. "Did we do a gut job, Mammi?"

"You did a wonderful gut job," she said, hugging him. Grinning, he ran out to join his cousins. She watched, her heart swelling. Lige was turning into a typical little boy—more so every day. This life was what he'd needed. He finally felt secure.

When she turned her attention back to the others, she found Daniel gesturing to the few existing cabinets. "I'd like to extend the cabinets all along this wall, and we talked about putting a few more on the end wall, as well." He grinned. "You should hear the Englisch ladies talk about the cabinet space when I work on their kitchens. Everything has to be pullouts and turntables and such. But Rebecca just wants regular cabinets, only more of them."

"Yah, and you could put one tall one in to store

brooms and mops and such. That's what I've been wanting, and Sam keeps promising."

It was time she interrupted before they had her whole kitchen mapped out for her. "I'm not going on with it right away, remember, Daniel?" She gave him a warning look. He'd better not say anything about her money problems.

"Just doing a little planning, that's all," he said in that easygoing way of his. "We don't have to start right away, but planning is half the work of the project. Makes it a lot easier once I actually start work."

Rebecca had a feeling he was manipulating her, but there didn't seem to be anything she could say. She couldn't stop him from thinking about the job, could she?

"Ach, I hear a buggy already," Leah exclaimed. "And me with the coffee not on yet. Here, Mary Ann, take that tray out. Rebecca, you'd best get the door unlocked. You have customers."

Her stomach fluttering, Rebecca rushed to the front door, unlocking it and setting it ajar before the first visitors had time to get to it. Ready or not, the quilt shop was open.

What was she thinking? Of course she was ready. This was what she'd been working toward, after all. Now the time was here.

As usual, her mother had been right. The steady flow of friends, neighbors, people from the church district… It seemed they'd all planned to stop by early, just to meet and greet and to wish her well. They headed gratefully toward the coffee and treats, and she was thankful to see that mothers steered their young ones out onto the front porch with their treats.

The last thing she'd want was sticky fingerprints on the new fabrics.

Somewhat to her surprise, one of the early visitors was Lydia Schultz, who had clearly been talking about her that Sunday after worship. She'd managed to avoid the woman since then, but inevitably they'd run across each other in their small community. It was too bad she hadn't remembered earlier that Lydia had a cousin who'd belonged to a neighboring church district to theirs out west.

Not that it would have made a difference if she had. If folks were inclined to gossip, they would do it, whether they had a reason to or not. Pinning a smile on her face, she went to greet Lydia.

"How nice of you to stop by our opening, Lydia. Will you have some coffee?"

Lydia, looking uneasy, shook her head. "I just thought I'd stop by and pick up some batting for the crib quilt I'm making. You do have it, don't you?"

"Yah, of course. Let me show you…"

"I'll do it, Aunt Rebecca," Mary Ann said quickly, appearing at her elbow. "I know just where it is." Showing a surprising amount of poise, she led Lydia off.

Rebecca turned to Leah, who was making an effort to appear busy. "Did you set that up?" she said in an undertone.

"Maybe," Leah admitted. Then her smile broke through. "No sense in giving Lydia a chance to pump you. Whatever you said would be twisted out of recognition by the time she repeated it, ain't so?"

"I gather Lydia has a reputation." Her momentary

queasiness at seeing the woman had vanished. If folks wanted to talk, she couldn't stop them.

"Ach, she's the worst blabbermaul in the county," Leah said. She shot a glance around to make sure no one had heard. "I guess I'm just as bad if I talk about her, ain't so?"

"Maybe not quite," Rebecca said, teasing.

Grateful as she was for the support of the church, by midmorning Rebecca was starting to feel a little overwhelmed and maybe a bit embarrassed.

"Why is Edith Stoltzfus buying pot holders from us when everyone knows she makes them herself?" she murmured to Leah after one sale.

Leah didn't seem troubled in the least. "So what if folks are buying things they maybe don't need? They'll give them as gifts, and that's gut advertisement for the shop, ain't so?"

When Rebecca still looked troubled, Leah patted her. "You're getting hungry—that's what's wrong with you. You go back to the kitchen and have yourself a snack before you keel over. Your mamm and I will look after things here."

Rebecca couldn't deny that the butterflies in her stomach seemed to have been replaced by a chasm. She didn't think food had anything to do with her feelings, but she hadn't been able to eat much breakfast, so it wasn't a bad idea.

When she reached the kitchen, she found Daniel leaning against the counter, drinking a cup of coffee and eating a whoopie pie. She chuckled at the cream filling that decorated his chin.

"You look like you have a white beard. What are you doing still here?"

"Eating," he said, wiping the cream away with a napkin. "And sorting the boards and such that are left over from the work on the shop. I don't like it when I buy too much, but sometimes it's hard to estimate."

"I wouldn't worry. You can always use it up, can't you?" She poured herself a cup of coffee and cut a generous wedge of shoofly pie. "I couldn't eat at breakfast this morning," she said in explanation.

"Too excited, ain't so? It certain sure sounds like it's a big success with all those women chattering at once." He nodded toward the shop. The sound was a little muted here, but it came through. "Sort of like the henhouse when the feed goes in."

"Women from the church," she said in explanation. She frowned down at her coffee. "They're all buying things...even things I'm sure they don't need. I wish..."

"What?" Daniel said. He gave her a gentle smile. "You're in business now, Rebecca. You're supposed to be happy when folks buy what you're selling."

"I am. I just don't want them to feel they have to." Couldn't he understand that?

Daniel set his cup down and focused on her. "Look at it this way. When you go to a mud sale, you buy something even if maybe you don't need it right at the moment."

"That's different. A mud sale benefits the school, or the fire company."

"It benefits the community," he said, patient as always. "Your shop is part of the community. Folks want to see it succeed. The more businesses there are, even just on this road, the more people will come down here and maybe stop at Stoltzfus's farm for berries or

Edna Byler's place for homemade fudge or my sister-in-law Jessie's for baked goods. We're all in this together, ain't so?"

"I guess, when you put it that way, I understand. But I still think some of them are coming just because they want to help me."

"Nothing wrong with that. You came to my business in place of someone else's, ain't so? We all help each other."

She was forced to smile. "You always have an answer for everything, don't you? I don't remember you being so smart when we were kinder."

"Wisdom comes with age," he said. "Now, you get back to work and sell something."

Her doubts allayed, Rebecca headed back into the shop.

"It's going well, ain't so?" Leah straightened the display of quilted pot holders on the counter.

"Yah." Rebecca hesitated. "It's wonderful kind of the Leit to show up like this, but we need some Englisch customers to make a go of the shop."

"They'll be here. Just wait." Leah seemed confident.

And of course it didn't really matter whether Englisch customers came today or another day, as long as they came. But still…

However, it seemed Leah was right. By late morning, several cars had pulled into the improvised parking area behind the shop, and clusters of Englischers buzzed happily around the shop. Rebecca, Leah, Mamm and even Mary Ann were all kept busy answering questions.

Rebecca chanced to overhear Mary Ann explaining the pattern of a Tumbling Blocks quilt to two of the women. Her young niece had more poise than she did, it seemed, and she chattered away quite at ease.

"You see?" Leah took a moment away from the counter. "I told you we'd get Englisch customers. In the summer it will be even busier, because travelers will stop, too."

"That's right." A young woman with a baby in a carrier against her chest entered the conversation. "You should be sure your shop is listed in that little booklet the county puts out for visitors. We moved here just a month ago, and I've used that to find all kinds of things."

"That's a gut idea," Leah said. "We didn't think of that. I'm Leah," she added, "and this is Rebecca Mast. She owns the shop."

"I'm Shannon Wilbur." She leaned against the counter, looking a little tired. She was a slim, tiny young woman, and Rebecca didn't doubt that the weight of the sleeping baby was dragging on her shoulders. "I've seen your name on some of the quilts, haven't I?"

Rebecca nodded. "I made many of them, but other Amish women from the area made some, too."

"They're lovely." Shannon hoisted the baby a little, probably to relieve the pressure of the straps. "We have more room in our new house, and my husband suggested getting a locally made quilt, so we'll have something to remember if we move."

"You're thinking of moving already? Don't you like it here?" Leah sounded a little shocked.

Shannon's effort at a smile seemed a bit forced. "It's my husband's job," she explained. "He has to travel a lot, and the company transfers him where it needs him. I never used to mind moving, but with the baby..." She let that trail off, but Rebecca understood.

She tried to imagine what it must be like in a strange town with a small baby and a husband who traveled, but she couldn't quite manage it. When Lige was born, a day didn't pass without some relative stopping by to help out.

Leah, with a gesture, summoned Mary Ann to her side. "This is my oldest girl, Mary Ann. Why don't you let her mind the baby while you're looking around? She loves babies, and she has lots of experience."

"That's right," Rebecca chimed in. "Have some coffee and a snack and enjoy yourself. Your little girl will be fine."

"Betsy." Shannon smiled down at the sleeping baby. "If you're sure..." She looked at Mary Ann, who was already holding out her arms. "All right. Thanks." She handed the sleeping child into Mary Ann's arms, watching for a moment to see how Mary Ann handled her. Then, apparently reassured, she walked toward the refreshment table with a light step.

"That's a kind thought." Rebecca was about to say more when her mother approached with an older woman—an Englischer with a warm, friendly air.

"Here is my daughter, Rebecca. This is Mrs. Allen. She loves to quilt."

"Glenda, please." She smiled from Mamm to Rebecca. "Your mother and I met last year at the spring mud sale. Your shop is just what we needed here. Now I won't have to drive twenty miles every time I run out of thread or batting."

"I'm glad. If you think of any other supplies you'd like me to carry, be sure you let me know."

"Oh, I will." The woman chuckled. "Everyone knows how outspoken I am. But you have a nice selection. I'm sure you'll do very well."

Shannon had come back up to them in time to hear her, a cup of coffee in one hand and a cruller in the other. "I think so, too. I hope you'll consider having a quilting group that meets here. I belonged to one where I lived before, and it was such fun to sit and sew with others who were interested. And then we'd have a quilting whenever one of us had a project ready." Her face was alive with enthusiasm for the idea.

"That's a wonderful idea," Glenda broke in. "My goodness, yes. I'd join in a minute. And I know a few other women who'd be interested. Now, let me see. When would be the best time to meet?"

Rebecca opened her mouth to speak and then closed it again at a look from her mother. The two women were chattering away happily, discussing days and times as if it were all settled. She glanced at Leah, who was smiling.

"Let them do it," she said softly. "Glenda Allen will do all the organizing for you, and it will bring more people into the shop, ain't so?"

Rebecca had to nod. Of course it was just what the shop needed. She should have come up with the idea herself. "I might need a little help."

"You have that without asking." Leah clasped her hand warmly. "Your mamm looks eager to volunteer, and I'll help, too. Maybe we should have Mary Ann here to watch any babies who come with their mothers. She'd love it."

Rebecca nodded, thankful. Of course they would help. Her mother was nodding and smiling as Glenda consulted her about the idea, and Mary Ann's face was blissful as she cradled the sleeping baby.

Rebecca looked around the shop, mentally seeing it as it had been that first day when she and Daniel had begun planning. Now it buzzed with color and movement and the happy sound of women's chatter. Her shop was just as she'd dreamed it.

Daniel squatted down by the back porch of the shop to have a closer look at the steps. He'd waited until after closing time, not wanting to be in the way when folks were leaving. But he had a bad feeling about those steps, even though he'd replaced one rotten board.

The back door opened, startling him, and he thought Rebecca was equally surprised to see him.

"What are you doing still here?" She stood above him at the top of the steps, looking down with a little apprehension.

"I was going to say the same to you." He chuckled. "We certain sure surprised each other. I thought you'd left with the others."

A faint flush touched her cheeks. "I know they thought I was silly, but I wanted to be there by myself for a little bit."

With the pink in her cheeks, Rebecca looked more like the rosy-cheeked girl he remembered. "Just to be sure it's real, ain't so?"

"You understand." She sounded surprised.

He nodded, rising to his feet. "I felt the same when I opened my carpentry business." He hesitated, wondering whether she wanted to talk or to be on her way. "It was a gut day, yah?"

"It was. I know every day won't be busy, but today made for a fine start." She looked down at the steps. "You didn't tell me what you're doing. You already fixed the step that was broken."

"Yah, but I don't like the looks of the uprights underneath. They're starting to give, and I wouldn't want someone to get hurt."

"I can't afford..." she began, but he shook his head.

"You already have the materials needed, left over from the shop. It won't be much work either. I have to go out tomorrow morning to give an estimate on a job, but I can do it in the afternoon."

She still looked uncertain, and he squatted by the steps to gesture. "Just take a look under here, and you'll see what I mean."

Rebecca took a quick stride down, bending. Her foot hit a stone, making her stumble, and he grabbed her arm to steady her.

In an instant, it seemed as though time had stopped. Rebecca winced away from his grasp as if he'd struck her, her blue eyes darkening with fear.

"Rebecca." He said her name softly, hardly trusting himself to say more. He eased back from her, giving her space.

She turned away from him, her breathing rapid, and wrapped both arms around herself. "I'm sorry. I don't know what..." She let that trail off, probably seeing that the reason for her reaction was only too obvious.

Daniel had control of himself now. He wouldn't let the fury he felt toward James show. James was gone beyond the reach of anything humans could do, and

God would have the judging of him. It wasn't for a fallible man like him to judge.

But Rebecca... She couldn't go on like this, trying to hold on to her secret when it kept leaking out of her and hurting her all over again.

"Komm." *Gently, gently.* He didn't dare touch her, even to help her up. "Sit here with me on the step. It'll hold a bit longer." He couldn't quite manage to say the words as lightly as he intended.

"It's all right." She stood, still avoiding his gaze. "I should go home."

"James hurt you," he said flatly. "Do you think I can't see that? Did he hurt Lige, too?"

"No!" Her breath caught. "Not...not physically. But Lige was hurt, anyway, by his father's anger and the way he acted. I don't think I realized how much it affected him until I came home and saw him with Sam and Leah's kinder."

At least she wasn't pretending. "Do they know? Did you talk to them, to your parents?"

Rebecca put her hand to her forehead, shielding her face. "They guessed because of Lige. But I didn't... I don't want to tell them. It would hurt them."

"Ach, Rebecca, don't you think they would be imagining even worse. Just knowing he hurt you—"

"People hurt each other in all kinds of ways." She seemed suddenly weary. "And it wasn't James's fault."

Daniel struggled to control himself. "How could it not be his fault? He was a grown man, not a child."

"In a way, he wasn't. Grown, I mean." She rubbed her temple. "You have to know about it to understand. James... Well, he was always a bit quick-tempered. And daring, almost as if he enjoyed taking chances.

But that was all, until the accident he had injured his head. Afterward, it was like he couldn't control himself. The doctors explained it to me. They said the injury had affected his impulse control. He'd flare up at the least little thing."

"And hit you." That was what he couldn't get past. He clenched his hands into fists despite his effort not to react.

"Not really hit." She pushed the word away, still trying to defend him. "He'd just grab me, push me… sometimes I'd fall." She shook her head. "I tried to get him to go back to the doctor. His parents tried. But he wouldn't listen. He didn't think there was anything wrong with him. It was everybody else who was at fault."

"If you'd left…" he began, knowing it was foolish even before he got the words out.

"He was my husband." There was dignity in Rebecca's answer, and he saw her draw on some inner strength.

"I know. You wanted to help him." Could she have had any love left for him by that time? Or had he killed it by then?

"Finally I went to the bishop. That seemed the only answer. And Bishop Paul was wonderful kind. He made all the arrangements for James to go into the hospital, to have the medication and counseling. He didn't give James a choice about getting it. And it seemed to help."

"So, you know you did the right thing in going to the bishop." He suspected there were a few people who'd call that disloyal. "It was the only thing you could do to help him recover."

Rebecca shrugged, seeming to find it easier to talk now that the worst was told. "Everyone didn't think so, but I had no choice but to act, for Lige's sake, as well as for James." She hesitated, her eyes darkening.

"What happened?" He longed to clasp her hand, but he controlled himself. "Something went wrong."

She nodded. "Maybe I counted on it too much. Maybe... Ach, I don't know. But one day, it all seemed to fall apart. He flew into a rage over a half-trained buggy horse, trying to force it into the harness. It reared up, hit him..." She pressed her lips together, but she didn't need to finish. He could see the outcome in her face.

"So that's how he was killed." He'd wondered, and now he knew.

Rebecca was silent, maybe even spent with the effort of telling her story. He wanted so much to put his arms around her and hold her close. To tell her...

What? There was little he could say or do. When she'd fallen as a child, he'd comforted her, but there was nothing he could do about this pain.

You can be her friend. His thoughts went back to Onkel Zeb's advice. That was what Rebecca needed right now. Not a new love, not someone to tell her what to do. Just a friend—a friend she could trust.

"It's over now." He picked his words carefully. "Lige is getting better, and you have a new life ahead of you."

"You won't tell anyone..."

Maybe she was regretting telling him already. "No, I won't tell anyone, though I think you should tell your mamm and daad the whole story. But it's up to you."

He hesitated, praying he was finding the right words. "I'm your friend, Rebecca. I won't speak unless you tell me to. You can always trust me."

Chapter Eight

Rebecca was just as glad not to see Daniel on Sunday. Maybe it was natural to feel regret and embarrassment after having told someone else something so personal.

But no, she didn't really regret it. The story had been ready to pour out of her, and Daniel was safe. She could trust him, and he wouldn't be as hurt by it as her mamm and daad would be. So the thing was done, but still, a break before she came face-to-face with Daniel was for the best.

Since it was an off Sunday for worship, the family had welcomed Aunt Ruth and Onkel Thomas and their children and grandchildren for the afternoon. Sam had cooked chicken on the grill; Mamm had baked, and she and Leah had prepared food for a whole host of folks. Naturally, Aunt Ruth and her daughters and daughters-in-law had insisted on bringing dishes, as well. The day had been filled with talk and laughter, and Lige had played with so many new cousins he'd lost count of them.

Now it was Monday, and Rebecca found the quiet shop a fine place to be, even though she'd only had one customer all morning. She still had some clearing up to do after the opening on Saturday, and she was engaged in planning how she would set up for the quilting group. The front corner of the shop would be ideal for that purpose, and she could set up a circle of chairs and a round table for folks to lay out fabric.

As she worked, she listened to the sound of voices filtering in from the back porch. Daniel had started work on the porch steps, and Lige had run eagerly to help him. Daniel's slow, deep voice contrasted with Lige's excited chatter, and both their voices were punctuated by the periodic sound of the hammer.

When had she heard Lige chattering like that to anyone but her? The thought seemed to touch her heart and resonate there. He was normally as silent as a little mouse, and though he'd begun to come out of his shell, he still didn't talk that freely to any adult except her. And now Daniel.

What a blessing it was to have come home again. James's parents hadn't wanted her to take Lige so far away, of course. That was only natural. But she thought they had understood, even though they didn't talk about it, how much Lige had been affected by his father's troubles. Perhaps this summer they'd come for a visit. She wasn't ready to take Lige back there yet, but eventually, maybe even that would be possible.

Busying herself with getting out books of quilt patterns for the group to see, she lost track of time, but eventually she realized that she wasn't hearing the voices from the back porch any longer, although the hammer still tapped. A vague uneasiness touched her, and she put down the book of quilt patterns and went back through the kitchen. No harm in leaving the shop unattended for a few minutes—she'd hear if a car or buggy pulled in.

Daniel still knelt by the steps, fitting a board into place, but Lige had wandered off into the yard. He knelt in the grass, seeming to concentrate on something.

Daniel finished what he was doing and looked up with a smile. "Are you taking a break?"

His relaxed expression bridged the faint awkwardness of the moment, and she was grateful. "Just a short one. You seem to have lost your helper."

"He'll be back. We noticed how many violets are blooming, and he decided to pick some for you. Hush, it's a secret."

"I promise to be surprised." She watched him return to his work, appreciating the skilled way he fitted each plank into place. He never hurried—each one had to be right before he moved on.

That reminded her of the appointment he'd been out on this morning. "How did your meeting go with the people who want their kitchen done? Did you get the job?"

"I don't know yet." He grinned. "The truth is the two of them haven't agreed yet on what they want. Everything I suggested, either the wife agreed and the husband didn't, or it went the other way around. I finally had to tell them I couldn't give an estimate if I didn't know what the job entailed."

"Usually it's the wife who has the final say about a kitchen," she said. "After all, she's the one who'll be working in it."

"Not with these two. It seems the husband prides himself on being a chef, and he wants everything organized just so. And his wife seemed more interested in having the latest style. Somehow I don't think it's going to end up being the right job for me."

That didn't seem to bother Daniel. "If she's so concerned about fashion, it wonders me that they'd call in an Amish carpenter to begin with, in that case," she said. "You'd think an Englisch company would be more to her taste."

"Oh, but the woman said having an Amish-built kitchen is all the rage now. Good workmanship and all that."

"That's true enough." It was just what she'd been thinking about him. "They couldn't do better than to hire you."

Daniel stopped working, sitting back on his heels. "The truth is that I'm not all that eager for the job. I have enough work to go on with, and I don't need something that might be a constant hassle." His smile was back, crinkling his eyes. "I don't want to be an umpire."

She laughed. "I don't blame you." For a moment they were silent, smiling at each other, and then Rebecca gave herself a mental shake. "I'd better get back to my work and let you get back to yours."

Escaping to the kitchen, she reminded herself that Daniel was a friend. Just a friend. That was all he wanted and all she wanted, as well.

She took a step toward the shop, and as she did, she heard Daniel shout loud enough to make her wince.

"Lige! Stop!"

Heart pounding, she ran back to the porch, jumped over the steps and raced toward her son. Lige stood by a pile of old boards lying next to the shed, seeming frozen to the spot, his small face white with fear.

Reaching him, Rebecca knelt to wrap her arms around him and hold him close. "It's all right," she crooned. "Nothing is wrong. You're safe."

She glared at Daniel, who'd come up beside them with a hoe in his hand. "How could you?" The words tumbled out, angry and unforgiving. "You know how he feels. I trusted you, and then you...you behaved just like James."

Daniel's face didn't change at the battering of her words. He took a step toward the pile of rotten wood and raised the hoe. The sun glittered for a moment off the blade as it flashed down.

Daniel struck again. Then, using the hoe, he lifted something from the woodpile and dropped it on the grass, safely distant from them. It was a copperhead.

Cold settled into Rebecca's heart. What had she done? She had to speak, to tell Daniel she was sorry...

But he ignored her, not even looking at her. He knelt next to her son and spoke softly.

"I'm sorry if I scared you, Lige. I didn't want to yell, but I had to. I was afraid that if you moved any closer, the copperhead might be startled." He touched Lige's back with a gentle hand. "Did you ever see a copperhead up close?"

Somehow the soft voice seemed to break through Lige's fear. He let go of Rebecca's skirt, looked at Daniel and then shook his head.

"Do you want to?" he asked. "It can't hurt you. It's dead now." He held out his hand. "Komm. Have a look."

Rebecca wanted to grasp her son and hold him

back, but she knew instinctively that would be the wrong thing to do. He was responding to Daniel, and there was a lesson to be learned right now. She couldn't interfere.

Lige hesitated. He looked up at her, and she managed to give him a nod and a smile. "Go ahead."

Her son reached out, and Daniel's large hand wrapped around his securely. Together they approached the snake. Daniel began showing Lige the markings, describing the hourglass pattern. She tried to watch, but tears stung her eyes.

She couldn't stand here any longer. She had to leave before they saw her cry. With a murmured excuse, Rebecca fled for the shop.

But even there, she couldn't be alone. Mamm was there waiting for her.

"Mammi." Rebecca turned away, trying to hide her tears. Her mother's arms went around her, and her mother's hands wiped her tears away.

"Hush, now, hush. It will be all right. Mammi's here."

The words calmed her as nothing else could. They were the words her mother had used when she was a small child—the same words she used when Lige was hurting.

Rebecca straightened, blinking back the last of her tears. "How...how did you get here? Why didn't I see you?"

Mammi took a step back, but her faded blue eyes still watched Rebecca with tender care. "You and Daniel seemed to be having words. I didn't want to interrupt, so I slipped in through the front."

"Maybe it would have been better if I had been

interrupted." She managed a shaky laugh. "I made such a fool of myself. Worse, I hurt Daniel—hurt him terribly. I don't know if he'll ever forgive me."

"There's nothing so bad it can't be forgiven," Mamm said. "You know that, and I'm sure Daniel does, as well." She hesitated. "Do you want to tell me about it?"

Rebecca's heart hurt that her mother felt she had to be so careful around her. What had she and Daad been imagining? They couldn't help but see that something had been wrong with her marriage…the marriage they hadn't wanted her to hurry into. Had they, even then, had doubts about James?

Rubbing her forehead, she tried to focus. Her head was aching from the thoughts and regrets that spun around her. She had to tell Mamm something.

"I heard Daniel yell at Lige. I didn't realize what was happening…just jumped into thinking it was like…like James all over again. I'm not even sure what I said to him, but I know I hurt him. And here, all along, he was just trying to protect Lige."

Her throat seemed to close at the thought.

Mamm touched her arm. "What did Lige need protecting from? Is he all right?"

"Yah, he's safe. It was a copperhead in that pile of old lumber by the shed. Daniel killed it. There's no danger."

"Ach, I told your daad that he and Sam should clean up back there." Mamm's voice took on a scolding tone, and Rebecca thought she was relieved to concentrate on something she could fix. "Well, they're going to do it before they're much older, I'll tell you that."

"Don't scold them too much." Her smile came more

easily now. "We've all had so much to do, and I...I haven't exactly been acting as if help is wilkom."

Mamm patted her. "We're family. We help each other. You just got a little...a little shortsighted for a bit."

Rebecca wasn't sure *shortsighted* was a strong enough word for it. She seemed to be seeing herself through her mother's eyes, and she didn't like what she saw.

She had let what happened with James change her deep inside herself. She'd turned into someone afraid to trust, afraid to open up even to those who loved her.

It wasn't a pretty picture, was it? Worse, she wasn't even sure she could change. It was one thing to recognize her fault, but another entirely to become again the woman she should be.

But at least she could begin to mend fences with her family easily enough, just by letting them help when they wanted to. Daniel was going to be more difficult.

"I have to tell Daniel how sorry I am. I have to ask his forgiveness."

"Yah, you do." Mamm glanced toward the back, where the duet of male voices could be heard again. "Wait a bit, maybe. Let him and Lige have some time together. Then you can talk to Daniel. He won't be building up a grudge, and you'll know when it's the right time."

Rebecca let her mother's words sink in, trying to believe she'd know when the time was right. And praying that, when it was, she'd be able to find the words.

Daniel forced himself to focus on Lige, blocking off the memory of Rebecca's angry words. Right now he couldn't do anything about Rebecca, but he could reassure Lige and bring him back to where they'd been before the incident.

His calm explanations seemed to bear fruit. Together they had taken the snake and tossed it into the deep weeds at the edge of the mowed yard.

Lige stood, staring at the spot. "Should we dig a hole and put it in?"

"We can do that." Would that reassure the boy? He was in over his head now, never having been a father and trying to think what Caleb would do in these circumstances. "But if we leave it there, it will scare mice and moles away from the yard. Mammi wouldn't like mice in her shop, would she?"

"Mammi doesn't like mice at all." Lige's small, serious face relaxed into a smile. "So that's a gut plan." He seemed satisfied, so Daniel let it go, hoping the boy wasn't in for a nightmare about snakes.

"I'd better get back to work on the steps. Do you want to help me?"

Lige nodded. "I'll hold the boards for you. Then I can tell Grossdaadi that I'm learning about making steps." He skipped on ahead to the steps and then circled back. "Grossdaadi is gut at teaching me how to do things. But so are you."

It was a generous compliment, Daniel decided. "Denke. Let's see if we can get finished."

Returning to the steps, they worked without saying much for a few minutes. Then Lige gave him a solemn look. "My daadi got kicked by a horse, and he died. If I got bit by a snake, would I die?"

Once again, Daniel was in way over his head. But the boy had asked him, and a question deserved an answer. "No, you wouldn't die. I'm right here, and I'd get the doctor to give you some medicine to make you better. You might feel sick for a while, though."

"Oh." He pondered Daniel's words. "I don't like medicine. But Mammi says sometimes we have to take it anyway."

"That's right." He tapped the final step into place. "I never could figure out why it has to taste so bad, though. What about you?"

Lige actually giggled. "Me, too. Mammi always gives me a drink afterward to take the taste away."

"Gut idea." His heart had warmed at the sound of that giggle. Lige would be all right.

As for Rebecca…who could say if or when she'd be all right? Her explosion at him had hurt him, not just because of what she'd said, but because it showed how far she had to go in recovering. The girl he'd known was gone, and he wasn't sure how to help the person she'd become.

He and Lige finished and packed up his tools. "Denke. I was wonderful glad to have your help."

"Me, too." Lige jumped off the new step. "I'm going to ask Mammi if I can go find Grossdaadi." He scrambled back up the steps and darted into the house.

Daniel hesitated. Should he leave? Or should he wait around, on the chance he could have a word with Rebecca? Not that he knew what he'd say if it happened.

He was still there when Lige ran back out, waved and trotted down the lane. Rebecca came out of the house, crossed the porch and walked slowly down the steps, looking everywhere but at him.

At the bottom, she stopped. "You made a wonderful gut job of the new steps."

"Lige and I," he amended. "I couldn't have done it without him."

"Ach, Daniel, you are so kind to him." She looked at him, her eyes filled with misery. "And, in return, I said such terrible things to you. Please, can you forgive me? There's no excuse. I just…"

She seemed to run out of words, but he knew what she was thinking. "You just felt as if you and Lige were back in the past. I understand."

"Do you?" Rebecca's expression was rueful. "I don't see how you can. You would never be so thoughtless and mean as I was."

"Rebecca, it was not such a terrible thing as you are making it." He almost took her hand but stopped himself.

"I hurt you." Her lips trembled on the words, and she pressed them together.

"Yah, I was hurt." He couldn't very well deny it. "But I knew what was happening. I understand."

Tears glistened in her eyes, but she smiled. "You always do understand. That's what makes you such a wonderful gut friend."

Friend, he reminded himself. All he could be to her was a friend, but that was what she needed. He had to keep telling himself that, so he wouldn't give in to the longing to put his arms around her.

"If you need to hear me say it, I forgive you," he said, keeping his tone light and teasing.

"Denke." She hesitated, and the worry came back into her face. "Now I have to explain it to Lige. I don't know what he must think."

Daniel thought of the child's questions and comments. "Lige may understand more than you might guess." He touched her hand, very lightly, pleased when she didn't pull away. "It will be all right. He'll understand that you were frightened for him. And that you love him."

"I hope so." She turned her hand, clasping his for a brief instant before turning away. "Denke, Daniel."

He stood, watching her as she walked away toward the farmhouse. His hand was still warm where she'd touched it, and he was smiling for no reason at all.

Chapter Nine

By the next morning, Rebecca had decided that she should take a step forward in conquering her fear of letting people in. Standing where she was didn't seem to be an option, and she'd seen the proof of Daniel's advice in the pleasure the family had taken in helping with the shop's opening.

At the moment, they were cleaning up the kitchen after breakfast, and the men and younger kinder had scattered to their chores. She brought a platter to the sink, where Mary Ann was washing dishes and Leah was drying.

"I was thinking about the quilting group coming this afternoon. You did say that you'd like to help, Leah. Do you think you have time today to sit in on it? I'm not sure how experienced any of them are, other than Mamm's friend."

Leah's face lit with a smile. "Ach, I was planning to get in on the group today. I'm looking forward to it. I can bring a table runner I'm working on, just so I have some reason for being a part of it."

"Why would you need a reason? You're working

with me on the shop, remember?" It was easy to see that Leah was genuinely pleased and not just pretending in order to be helpful.

"Can't I do something, Aunt Rebecca?" Mary Ann turned, her hands full of soapsuds. "I can help any customers who come in while you're busy. And if the lady with the boppli is there, I could watch the little one for her."

She glanced at Leah for her approval, and Leah nodded.

"Denke, Mary Ann. I'm pretty sure she's coming, so that would be helpful."

"Shannon doesn't seem to have any close friends or family here in the valley," Leah said. "That's a shame. It's not easy to manage everything, especially with a first baby." She smiled and flicked her dish towel at her daughter. "That wasn't you, you know. I made all my mistakes on your brother."

"I'll tell him so the next time he starts bossing me." Mary Ann's eyes twinkled, making her look very like her mother.

"You'll never break a big brother of that," Rebecca said. "Your daadi was my big brother, and he still thinks I need his help and advice, just because he claims he held my hand when I-was learning to walk."

Leah shook her head in mock sorrow. "Poor Sam. We'd best not tell him we were talking about him."

Rebecca nodded, but the light words made her wonder if she'd hurt her brother's feelings when she didn't seem to need him. There seemed to be no end to the possible wrong steps she could take with those who loved her.

"How many women do you think will be there this

afternoon?" Leah dried her hands and hung up the towel. Together they finished putting dishes back in the cabinet.

"I wish I knew. Probably at least three, but from what Mamm's friend said, she intended to tell others about it."

"Glenda Allen," Leah said, supplying the name. "Glenda likes to organize things, that's certain sure. I guess they'll bring their own supplies, but it wouldn't hurt to have a few extra needles and such ready."

"I'll get some out once I open the shop this morning."

Leah stood with her hand on the cabinet door, as if she had something on her mind. Finally she turned to Rebecca with her quick smile.

"I'm wonderful glad you asked me to be a part of the shop. I know you've said you wanted to stand on your own feet since James's death, and I didn't think I should push. But I wanted to, like I always do." She gave a little laugh, as if admitting a fault she wasn't really sorry for.

"I'm glad, as well." She clasped Leah's hand in an impulsive movement. "I've been a little silly about that. Anyway, that's what Daniel says."

"So you'll take advice from Daniel, will you?" Leah's tone was teasing. "I might have known. Sam says the two of you were always telling each other your secrets when you were small."

"We did." She frowned a little. Was that still appropriate, to be so close when they were grown?

"Now, don't start worrying about it," Leah said, seeming to read her thoughts. "Daniel is a friend." She darted a quick, teasing glance at her. "Maybe some-day he'll be more."

Before Rebecca could deny it, Leah had whisked out the back door, calling to one of the children.

Rebecca stood where she was, seeing what had been hidden from her until this moment. Daniel had moved from being her childhood friend to being some-one whose presence and support was necessary to her happiness.

That frightened her, because she'd promised herself she'd never lean on a man again. And more important, because Daniel had never given a sign that he wanted anything more than friendship from her.

It was nearly time for the quilting group to gather, and Rebecca was a bundle of nerves. Could she really pull this off? Leah, who must have been interpreting her expressions, gave her a quick hug.

"You'll do fine. Everyone is coming to quilt, not to judge."

"You're right. I'm being foolish, I suppose, but…" She stopped when the bell over the door jingled, sur-prised because she hadn't heard a car.

It was Jessie, Daniel's sister-in-law, and she car-ried a workbasket. "This is the right time, yah? Leah told me about the quilting group, and I'd like to join."

She looked a little uncertain, and Rebecca hurried to make her welcome. "I'd sehr be glad for you to join us. I don't know how much the Englisch ladies know about quilting, though."

"That's fine." Jessie set down her basket in order to remove her bonnet and pat her hair into place.

She was about Rebecca's age, Rebecca thought,

with a serene, pleasant face and that glow women had when they were expecting a baby. For just an instant, Rebecca envied that joy. Would she ever experience it again?

Leah had mentioned once that Caleb's first wife, Jessie's cousin, had been a beauty. No one would say that about Jessie, she supposed, but Jessie radiated kindness in a way that drew people to her.

"Caleb thinks I need to get out and do things with other women. He's always worrying I'll feel out of place so far from my family. I tell him it's nonsense, but he worries." A slight shadow crossed her face, and Rebecca wondered if she were thinking about her cousin.

"Caleb loves you, that's all." Leah said, smiling. "I'm glad he thinks of things like that, especially if it means you'll join us."

A car sounded on the gravel outside, and in a moment, another one. In a few minutes, the shop was filled with the sound of women's voices.

Shannon had been the first one there, and she willingly surrendered little Betsy to Mary Ann. "Thanks so much. There's a bottle in the diaper bag if she seems hungry. And you can always hand her back to me if she's fussy."

"We'll be fine." Mary Ann bounced the baby adeptly. "Betsy remembers me. Don't you, Betsy?"

The baby cooed up at her, for all the world, as if she were agreeing, and the other women laughed.

"Relax," Glenda said. "Amish girls seem to be born knowing how to handle babies. Every young mother needs a respite now and then. I still remember how my back would ache from walking the floor with a fussy baby."

The friend she'd brought with her—a woman about her age that she'd introduced as Alice—shook her head. "Being with my babies was the happiest time of my life. I wouldn't have traded a second of it."

Shannon, hearing her, looked a little abashed, as if she'd been a bad mother for handing her baby over to someone else, even for a moment.

Then the third Englischer, Debby, a woman with a dark, lively face and a wealth of dark curls, gave a chuckle. "Alice, you know perfectly well you're looking back at those days through rose-colored glasses now that your children are all grown and gone. Believe me, I have three school-age boys, and sometimes I'd give a million bucks just for a little peace and quiet."

"Shut yourself in the bathroom," Glenda said and looked surprised when everyone laughed. "I'm serious. When my kids were little, that was the only place I could go that they wouldn't come looking for me."

Somehow that frank admission seemed to break the ice, and Rebecca was able to get everyone settled in the area she'd set up for them. In a few minutes, each of the women had brought out a project and started comparing notes about quilting techniques.

Listening carefully, as she nodded and smiled, Rebecca realized that Glenda was probably the only advanced quilter in the group. She and Leah would need to spend a little time showing techniques as they went along.

Shannon took out a fairly simple Log Cabin square that was, she said, intended for a table runner. "I took a class the last place we lived, and that's where I started it. But then we had to move, and I didn't get to finish the project."

"Well, you can do it now," Leah said. "If there's anything that you don't understand, just speak up. Someone will have an answer."

Glenda nodded in agreement. "It must have been hard moving when your baby was so small."

Shannon shrugged. "It's Rick's job," she said. "He's a sales representative, and the company keeps transferring him where they need him. It wasn't so bad at first…kind of exciting, really, to see new places. But now…"

"Things are different when you have a baby," Rebecca finished for her when she seemed reluctant to say the words. "I remember when my Elijah was small, and we lived out in Ohio. My husband's family was kind and helpful, but I longed for my mother and my cousins, even so."

The other women began sharing their own experiences, and soon they were chattering as if they were old friends, while their needles flashed through the fabric. It was like an Amish quilting frolic, Rebecca realized.

Maybe the point was that women were women, no matter whether they were Englisch or Amish. If they'd had or were going to have babies, they had a common bond that brought them together.

Glenda spread out the crib quilt she was working on—a lovely applique pattern in pastel colors, with teddy bears and puppies. "This is for the new grandbaby we expect to see in September."

They all oohed and aahed about it, and it just confirmed Rebecca's opinion that Glenda was an excellent quilter. So good, in fact, that it wondered her why Glenda had been eager to belong to a group. But maybe she, like Shannon, enjoyed the companionship.

"This will be ready for quilting by next week." Glenda looked from Leah to Rebecca. "Do you want to have everyone participate in the quilting?"

"That would be fun," Debby exclaimed. "Could we?"

"For sure. If everyone agrees, I'll have a quilting frame set up." Rebecca glanced around the room. She'd have to move a few things to fit her quilting frame in so they could all sit around it. "I'll get everything ready for next week."

Jessie was looking at the available space, as well. "If you want, you can use my portable quilting frame. It would be plenty big enough for a crib quilt, and easier to bring in, I think."

"That would be wonderful, if you're sure you won't need it yourself."

Jessie shook her head. "I don't have anything nearly ready for quilting."

"It's all set then."

Glenda obviously enjoyed having things settled. She smoothed the crib quilt with her palm.

"I have a crib quilt that was made for me by my grandmother. Now I'm making one for my expected grandchild. That's nice, isn't it? To think how women's handiwork passes on from one generation to the next."

They all nodded, touched, but it was Shannon who spoke. "I have one, as well. That was really what got me started in quilting. My grandmother said she sewed love into every stitch."

Rebecca felt tears sting her eyes. The two Englischers, between them, had said exactly what she felt about quilting, women and love.

Daniel ran his hand along the curve of the back piece for the rocking chair he was making. Jessie, he felt sure, would love it even if there were flaws, but he wanted the gift to be perfect—or at least as near perfection as he could make it. No craftsman could ever claim that something he'd made was perfect.

The door to his workshop opened, and he looked up, startled to see Rebecca linger on the step, as if not certain of her welcome. But surely they'd put the discomfort of her explosion behind them.

"Rebecca, komm in. What brings you here?" He sent a quick look around the room, wishing it looked a little neater. But it was a workshop, not a parlor, after all.

"Jessie said…" She stopped, smiling a little. "I'm starting backward, I guess. Jessie came to the quilting group today, and she mentioned a portable quilting rack I could borrow. To use in the group, you see. I'm sure I could have carried it, but she said you could bring it when you come over the next time."

"I'd be glad to bring it. Jessie probably wants to make sure it's spotless before it goes over to your shop."

"Maybe so." She moved a bit closer. "What are you working on? A new kitchen job?"

"Ach, no, not now." Daniel stepped out of the way so she could see the half-finished rocker. "It's for Jessie. What do you think?"

"She's going to love it." Rebecca smoothed her hand

along the back, much as he had done. "I didn't realize you made furniture as well as doing remodeling."

"A little bit of everything, I guess," he admitted. "I haven't made a rocker before, but Onkel Zeb helped me with shaping the rockers. That's the only thing that was tricky."

"You wouldn't want it to creak and wobble when she's rocking in it."

Rebecca's smile was sweet as she looked at it, as if she were remembering rocking her own little one, and it touched his heart. Of course, they both knew Jessie needed the rocker because she was going to have a baby, but custom insisted that babies weren't talked about in mixed company, until they were safely in their cradles.

She would leave in a moment, her message delivered, and he found he didn't want her to go.

"How did the quilting group go this afternoon? Were you pleased with it?"

"Oh, yah, so happy." Rebecca smiled, shaking her head a little. "I don't know what I was worried about. Englisch or Amish, women are interested in the same things. We chattered away as if it were an Amish quilting frolic."

"See? I knew it would work out. And having the group will draw people to the shop."

"That's what Leah said. Quilters will hear about us and want to buy their supplies at our shop. I'm thinking we could do just as much business with fabrics and notions as with the quilts and such."

"More business maybe, but not more money. Some people will drive miles to find a handmade quilt, so I've heard. I was thinking about that—you need to get listed in that little booklet about things to see and do in the county."

"Actually, Shannon, the one who has the baby, mentioned that on the day I opened the shop, and reminded me again when she was leaving the quilting group. One of the others said she'd take a picture of the shop and send it in for me on her computer. Wasn't that kind?"

He nodded, thinking other people besides him found Rebecca an easy person to be kind to. "It wouldn't be a bad idea to put up some signs, too. Pretty soon you'll have as much business as you can handle."

"I don't know about that, but I'm wonderful happy to think that I'll be able to support my son with my business. And besides, it's just what I've always wanted to do."

"To be able to work at something you love is a gift," he said soberly, thinking of the times when he'd thought himself destined to spend all his life working the dairy farm, until Caleb's son was old enough to help more.

"I can't tell you how much I appreciate what you've done." Rebecca reached out impulsively but stopped short of touching him. "I'd never have done it without your help."

"You would have. You've turned into a strong woman, Rebecca."

It was true. He didn't know why he should be surprised at that. Despite all the unhappiness she'd endured in recent years, she'd come through it with her inner self still strong. Maybe she didn't recognize it entirely herself yet, but she would, in time.

Rebecca didn't seem to know what to do with

his words. After a moment, she shook her head just slightly. "Denke, Daniel. I'm not so sure about it myself, but I'm grateful I've been able to count on you."

Her words seemed to hit him right in the heart. Could anyone really count on him? "I wish…" he began and then let the words fade away.

"You're thinking of Aaron, ain't so?" Rebecca's eyes filled with sympathy.

"How did you know?" he asked, somewhat reluctantly, not sure he wanted to talk about his brother.

"There's a look on your face when you think of him—love and hurt mixed up together." She hesitated before going on, maybe wondering if she was going too far. "Have you heard anything more of him?"

"No. Onkel Zeb says we just have to wait and pray that Aaron will decide to return to us. I guess we can't make the decision for him. But it's awful hard to do nothing now that I know where he is."

Rebecca was silent for a moment, frowning a little. "I wouldn't want to argue with Zeb, but…" She paused again. "You know, after James died, I got sort of stuck. I couldn't make up my mind which way to turn, and everyone else was telling me what to do. And then Mamm and Daad came. They didn't try to decide for me. They just let me know that a home was waiting for me and Lige here. I think maybe I needed to hear that from them."

Daniel let her words sink in, and they resonated in his heart. Could it be true? Was it possible that Aaron needed to hear that his home was waiting for him?

If so, they had to tell him.

Chapter Ten

Rebecca moved around the shop, putting away things she'd got out for the quilting group the previous day. She now had the portable quilting rack against one wall, and she didn't want the shop to start looking cluttered.

Daniel had shown up early with the quilting frame, but then he'd left, saying he had some things to do. That was just as well. If she found him working on her house again, she'd have to tell him to stop. She couldn't let him continue working without pay.

There might have been another reason for Daniel's quick disappearance this morning. Had he been disturbed by what she'd said when he'd talked about Aaron? It was certainly possible. She'd tried not to give advice, but to stick to what had helped her when she was far from home. But maybe, even that was unwarranted interference. Daniel was very sensitive about what he saw as his failure with his little brother. She certainly hadn't wanted to make him feel even worse.

And now that she considered the circumstances, it

had probably wondered him why she was in his workshop at all. There hadn't been any very good reason for it. Jessie could have passed the word along herself.

The truth was that Jessie was matchmaking, she feared, just as Leah was. Oh, they were being careful. They probably thought they'd been very subtle, but she'd seen through them quickly. They thought she and Daniel would make a good pair.

Maybe they would have at a different time, but not now. Not when Daniel was tied in knots over his perceived failure with people he'd loved, and not when she felt it impossible to trust her future and Lige's to another man. If only…

A futile line of thought was broken when a car pulled in by the shop. Rebecca gave a quick brush to her apron and pretended to be busy sorting the thread rack.

The bell jingled, and a tall well-dressed Englisch woman came in. Not just well-dressed, but maybe a bit over-dressed for the country. She'd look more at home on a city street, Rebecca considered. Not local, that was certain.

She smiled and moved toward the woman. "Wilkom. May I show you something?"

The woman looked around, frowning a little, before speaking. "I'm interested in full-size quilts. What do you have in stock?"

"This way." Rebecca led her to the bed she'd set up to display some of the full-size quilts. They were spread out on the bed, one on top of the other, so the customer could see how each one looked. "Were you interested in any particular color or pattern?"

"No, not really." She stared at the classic Nine-Patch

quilt that was on top, running her hand along it, leaning close to examine the stitching, examining the back and then flipping up the tag on the corner that listed the price and the maker.

Then she jotted a couple of notes in a small notebook she took from her handbag. "The price is a little high for a simple nine-patch, don't you think?" Without waiting for an answer, she went on. "Let's see the next one."

Rebecca carefully folded back the top quilt to reveal the one underneath. This quilt, one that she'd made herself, rather than one of those on consignment, was a Tumbling Blocks quilt done in rather bold colors. She'd felt a qualm or two about the colors herself, but she thought it was something that might appeal to an Englischer.

"Hmm." The woman obviously wasn't one to commit herself, but the sound seemed favorable. She went through the whole process again, just as she had with the first one, and jotted down information in that small notebook. Again, she frowned at the price.

"I might be interested, but the price is far too high," she said crisply. "Consider cutting it in half, and I'd think about it."

Rebecca was speechless for a moment. She'd told herself to expect rudeness at times from customers, but didn't the woman realize that what she'd suggested meant that Rebecca would receive pennies an hour for the work that had gone into the quilt?

Perhaps not. Or maybe she was just accustomed to bargaining for everything she bought.

"I couldn't do that," she said, trying to keep her voice firm. With a quick movement, she turned back the Tumbling Blocks quilt to reveal the Log Cabin quilt in shades of blue and yellow that one of Leah's friends had made.

The woman made a gesture, as if she'd pull the other quilt back, but she checked it. Instead, she studied the one in front of her with that same careful assessment.

Rebecca couldn't quite figure it out. She'd watched people buying quilts often enough, but they usually had a color scheme in mind and were looking for the perfect quilt to fit into it. They didn't usually jot down so many notes either, maybe just asking the prices on some they were interested in.

This woman was certainly a meticulous shopper. They went through the whole process with every quilt, and by the time they'd finished, Rebecca figured she'd probably filled up her entire notebook.

At last, frowning at what she'd written, she spoke abruptly. "Let me see the Tumbling Blocks quilt again."

Rebecca turned back, reminding herself that patience was a necessary requirement for a shopkeeper. "The Tumbling Blocks pattern depends upon the colors the quilter chooses to give the impression of movement in the design."

"Yes, I know. Did you make it?"

Rebecca nodded.

"Good, then you can negotiate the price," the woman said briskly. "I'll give you two hundred and fifty for it. Cash." She actually opened her purse and took out a roll of bills.

"I'm sorry." Rebecca resolutely turned her gaze away from the money and declined to think about what she could do with the money. This was a business, not a private matter. "I couldn't possibly."

"Come on now. You can't possibly get the price you have marked. You don't exactly have people lined up to buy your quilts. Isn't it worth it to you to make a sale and have some ready cash?" She began counting out the sum.

Somehow, the gesture was the last straw. It was rude in any culture. Rebecca wouldn't allow herself to become angry, but she suspected her cheeks were flushed.

"No. I couldn't think of it. The quilt is worth every penny of the price."

"It's only worth what someone is willing to pay for it," the woman replied.

True enough, but she wasn't going to give away the work of her hands that easily.

"I couldn't." A wave of annoyance swept through Rebecca. The Englischer looked ready to stand there and argue all day. "I might consider discounting the price a little, but I would have to discuss it with my partner first."

"I thought this was your shop." The woman's tone was sharp.

"It is, but I have a partner, and she's not here today." Leah was only as far away as the farmhouse, but there was no reason why she needed to know that. "If you'd care to come back another day, we can talk about it."

It took several repetitions of that statement, but finally she seemed to get through. The woman shoved her notebook into her bag, snapped the bag closed on notes and money and stalked out.

No sooner had she gone than Leah came rushing in

the back door, flushed and breathless. "That woman," she gasped. "You didn't let her talk you into anything, did you?"

"Of course not." Rebecca pushed away the thought of how tempting that cash had been. "She offered me a ridiculous price for the Tumbling Blocks quilt, and I turned her down. Why?" Obviously there was something going on that she didn't understand.

Leah leaned against the counter, getting her breath and laughing a little. "Oh, dear. How silly I must have looked, running down the lane like a loose pony. I recognized the car, you see."

"No, I don't see," she said, smiling at Leah's amusement. "Leah, what are you talking about?"

"That woman," Leah said. "I recognized the car, because I happened to see it at Elsie Schutz's house one day. Elsie said the woman is a dealer. She drives around the county buying up quilts as low as she can get them, and then offers them for three or four times that at a shop in the city. Elsie said I should warn you, but in all the fuss of getting open, it slipped my mind."

"Ach, so that's it." Rebecca leaned against the counter next to her, giggling a little and feeling weak in the knees at the same time. "I should have guessed, but I never thought of it. I figured she was just looking for a bargain. And maybe thinking she could get the better of a dumb Amish woman."

"So long as you didn't give in. That's the important thing. I was kicking myself when I realized I hadn't warned you and there she was already. Ach, I'm sehr sorry, Rebecca."

"Nothing to be sorry about." Rebecca patted her

arm. "It ended fine. I didn't let her take advantage of me."

She repeated those words to herself. No, she hadn't let the woman take advantage of her. Maybe she was regaining a little of the spunk she used to have after all.

Daniel had no sooner started removing one of the old cabinets from the kitchen wall than Rebecca erupted into the room from the shop.

"Daniel, what are you doing? I thought you understood we couldn't go on with the work until…" She glanced at Lige, looking at her with wide blue eyes, and seemed to change her mind about the end of that sentence. "Until later."

From his perch on the step stool, Daniel gestured to Lige. "That one," he said. "The biggest screwdriver."

Lige handed it up to him, eager to help.

"Please stop."

She sounded determined, and he suspected he was in for a battle. That was one reason he'd stopped at the farmhouse and picked up Lige. The other was that he just plain enjoyed being with the boy.

"All I'm doing is prep work right now," he said, attacking the old screws that were rusted into place. "I want to see what condition the wall is in behind this cabinet. Then I can be more realistic about the work I'm going to do."

"But you should be taking other jobs. I'm sure there are people who want your services. People who can… Who are in a position to…" Rebecca stopped, obviously not wanting to mention her lack of money in front of her son.

He couldn't help smiling, and she saw it. "I suppose you know there are things I can't say with little pitchers around."

Daniel's smile grew into a grin. "That's why I brought this one."

He moved on to the next screw. Given the shape they were in, this was going to take a while. He could just break up the cabinet, but it went against the grain to do that needlessly. A craftsman didn't just discard materials. If he could get it off in one piece, it might work in the cellar for Rebecca to store her canned goods.

Rebecca seemed to have stopped arguing, but her expression was somber as she watched him. Finally he sighed and climbed down from the stepladder. He turned to face her squarely. It looked as if they'd best have this out.

"Listen, here's the way it is. I really don't have any big jobs on hand right now. Just a few little things I can fit in here and there. I was meant to be starting work on a project this month, but it's been delayed, and nobody knows for how long. So I can't really start anything else big, because I have to be available when they need me."

"I see, but…"

"So you'd be doing me a favor by letting me fit this in now."

"It seems to me it's the other way around when it comes to favors," she said, her voice tart as a lemon.

"Ach, don't be foolish, Rebecca. I can wait to be paid later. What I can't do is two things at once. So let me get on with this while I'm free. And while I've got Lige to help me."

He tapped the top of Lige's straw hat, and Lige grinned.

"Yah, Mammi. Come September, I'll be in school, and I won't be here to help Daniel."

For a moment longer, she held out against him. Daniel saw the exact instant she gave in—when a tiny smile started in her eyes.

"All right, all right. I guess I can't argue with the two of you. But mind, if you get a chance to work on something else, you take it."

He nodded, feeling triumphant. Rebecca was never going to know whether he turned down another job to work on her house. He'd see to that.

Lige seemed to be losing interest in the adult conversation. He poked at the cardboard box Daniel had carried in with him.

"What's this, Daniel? It looks like plants."

"That's what it is, and I almost forgot to tell your Mammi about it. I'd be in trouble then." He bent and lifted the box to show Rebecca. "This is from Jessie. She saw that you were cleaning up the flower bed alongside the house, so she sent you starts from some of her plants."

"How kind of her." Rebecca came at once to peek into the box. "What did she send?"

Daniel had to shake his head. "To tell you the truth, I don't really remember. I'm not much of a hand for flowers. I just know they're pretty and they smell nice."

"Would they interest you more if they were made of wood?" She was burrowing through the box, and she didn't seem to have any trouble identifying them, just from the young shoots. "That's coreopsis, I'm sure. And coneflowers. And this looks like some type of daisy."

"Can we plant them, Mammi?" Lige bounced up and down at the thought of digging in the dirt. "Please?"

"Why don't we all do it?" Daniel said. "We'll come back to this later, yah? The plants should go in while they're fresh and green. And I see that Jessie even put some trowels in for us to use."

Lige grabbed his mother's hand, but Daniel thought she didn't really need much urging.

"I'll see the car or buggy if anyone comes, so I guess it's all right to leave the shop." She laughed as Lige tugged her along. "Okay, I'm coming."

The three of them trooped outside, with Daniel carrying the box. Planting flowers wasn't exactly part of his job, but he liked seeing the boy's excitement and Rebecca's obvious pleasure. If it were that easy to make her happy, he'd bring plants every day.

Lige, of course, wanted to plunge right in to putting something in the ground.

"Wait, now." Kneeling, Rebecca put out her hand to stop him. "We don't want to get too close to some things that are already here. See those yellow tulips? We'll go over a little more to put in these coneflowers."

"Why is it a coneflower, Mammi?" Lige seemed full of questions these days. Maybe that was a sign he'd started to feel safe here.

"That's a gut question." Daniel echoed, "Why is it a coneflower?"

"You think I don't know, don't you?" Her eyes laughed at him, and it was like old times. "It's because the seed heads in the middle of the blossom get so big they look like cones. The butterflies and birds love them."

Lige poked him. "See? Mammi knows everything about flowers."

That made them both laugh. "Maybe not everything," Rebecca said. "But I do know the coneflowers will spread out, so we have to give them space."

Lige began digging enthusiastically in the spot she indicated, and Daniel leaned across to help him. The soil was rich and friable, since the previous owners had planted there for years. "We'll watch the birds eating the seeds in late summer, ain't so?"

"Yah, we will." Lige's face clouded suddenly. "But what about next year? Will we see them then?"

"For sure." Rebecca was so quick to reassure him that Daniel realized she wanted him to know that this was their permanent home. "These flowers are perennials. That means they come back again, every single summer."

"Gut." Lige gave a little nod, the cloud disappearing from his face.

Daniel exchanged glances with Rebecca, and they shared a moment of understanding about her son. If only… He let that thought drift away. They were both satisfied with things the way they were between them. Why go looking for trouble?

They worked their way along the side of the house. Rebecca seemed able to visualize just where she wanted each plant, and what it would look like when it was in place. She had an eye for shape and color, he guessed. It came through in her quilts, and maybe it also applied to her flowers.

When they reached the end of the planting, Rebecca sent Lige to the outside spigot to rinse off the trowels. "We want to send them back to Jessie nice and clean, ain't so?" she added when he looked as if he'd balk at the chore.

Lige nodded, grabbing the trowels, and ran off happily enough. Rebecca continued to kneel, staring at the plants in front of her, clenching her hands in her lap. Finally she looked up at him.

"I'm thinking I should apologize for what I said yesterday. About your little brother, I mean. It wasn't any of my business, and I shouldn't..."

"Ach, stop." Impulsively he put his hand over hers. In the instant he had to be sorry he'd touched her unexpectedly, he realized Rebecca didn't wince or pull away. He breathed a little easier. "Of course it's your business. We're friends. I know you care about Aaron."

Her hand relaxed under his.

"I certain sure care about him." Her lips curved in a reminiscent smile. "I still see him as the little bruder who tagged along after us, teasing and wanting to do everything you did. And I care about you. I...I hate to see you hurting and blaming yourself for what Aaron did. But maybe your onkel Zeb is right."

"Maybe so. Yah, of course he is right that Aaron has to make the decision. But what if you were right, too? What if, like you, Aaron is waiting for someone to assure him that he still has a place here? That could be true, ain't so?"

"I guess so." Her gaze searched his face. "You've decided to do something. What is it?"

He had to laugh a little. "You always could read me like a book. Yah, I can't rest until I've done something. So I found out the name of that place where Eli Gaus said he was working. And this morning, I went to the library and used their computer to get the address."

"You're going to write to Aaron." Rebecca's blue eyes shone. "Daniel, I'm wonderful glad."

He found he loved having her look at him that way, with her face alight and her eyes shining. He couldn't get enough of that expression.

Slowly it began to fade, and a troubled one took its place. "But if he doesn't answer, you'll be hurt all over again. I don't want that to happen." She was actually holding his hand between both of hers, pressing it close between her palms, and he could hardly breathe for fear she'd realize what she was doing and pull away.

"It will still be better than knowing I didn't try when I could have." He looked down at their clasped hands, feeling as if he drew courage from her touch. "After you said what you did yesterday, I began to wonder. What if God was telling me something?"

She shook her head slightly. "What if it was just me saying too much?"

"No." The more he thought of it, the surer he was. "First there was Eli running into Aaron, and then his wife insisting he tell us, so we know where Aaron is. And then you saying that about needing to know you'd be wilkom if you came back home again. How could I ignore it if that was God's leading?"

"You couldn't. I see that now."

Her eyes met his. Emotions seemed to ripple between them—hope, joy, sorrow, longing—all mixed together. It was like a living thing stretched between them, linking them, stretching into both the past and the future.

His breath caught, his fingers tightening on hers. That was what life was, wasn't it? All those feelings and experiences coming at a person, good and bad mixed together. And if you were very fortunate, you had someone who cared, someone who felt them with you, sharing them.

He leaned toward Rebecca, irresistibly drawn. Her lips parted, the blue of her eyes seeming to darken. If only…

Then Lige came running back to them, the trowels clattering in his hand. Rebecca swung toward her son, and the moment was gone.

But it had happened, Daniel thought, watching the two of them chattering together. It had happened, and what were they going to do about it?

Chapter Eleven

Daniel hadn't found any answer to his question during a mostly sleepless night. Nothing had changed between him and Rebecca, and yet everything had changed.

How could it be? His love for her had changed from that of childhood playmates to the love between a man and a woman. It seemed sudden, and yet it must have been growing steadily, out of sight, but it burst forth like a plant breaking through the blanketing soil.

He'd eaten breakfast automatically, giving the wrong answers when anyone asked him anything and making his niece and nephew giggle when he nearly put sugar on his eggs. He had to get hold of himself. Onkel Zeb was already watching him with a question in his wise old eyes, and he'd see the truth too easily.

When they'd finished, Daniel made a quick escape and hurried to the workshop to gather any materials he might need today. Last chance, he told himself. This would never work, for reasons he knew only too well. He'd failed too many people that he loved. He couldn't possibly add Rebecca and Lige to the count.

Besides, Rebecca had problems of her own. After what she'd told him about her marriage, it didn't take much imagination to see what her response would be to the idea of marrying again. She'd never trust her and Lige's happiness to another person. She was probably already denying that anything had happened between them yesterday.

He was right back to where he'd been before. Rebecca and Lige needed a friend, nothing more. He was that friend, so he'd better get himself to work before they wondered where he was. But it wasn't going to be easy to be around Rebecca and behave normally.

As it turned out, he didn't have to be around her all that much. She was heading into the storeroom when he arrived, but she turned back for a moment.

"There, Lige, I told you Daniel would be here." She gave her son a little pat on the shoulder and glanced at Daniel, then away again. "He's ready to work. And I want to rearrange the storeroom, so I'll be back there. I don't expect anyone to come in the shop this early."

Daniel nodded. Was she a little wary of being with him this morning? Maybe, but if so, she seemed to be coping. "Okay, Lige. What say we get the rest of the old cabinets out today?"

"I'm ready." Lige tried to flex his muscles. "When are we putting up new ones?"

"I've been working on the new ones in my workshop, and they'll soon be ready. We might need to do some repair work on the walls before they go in."

"Let's get to work, then," he said, sounding so much like his uncle that it made Daniel smile in spite of his distraction.

The rest of the cabinets seemed to come off more

easily than the first one had. Lige, in a talkative mood, chattered about this and that, and Daniel could work and listen in amusement without difficulty. It sounded as if Lige was longing to be like his year-older cousin and go to school, but that would happen soon enough.

"Come September, and you'll be going off with the other scholars first thing every morning. What will I do for a helper then?"

Lige's small face grew serious. "I could help when I come home from school. And when I'm old enough, I could be your apprentice." He beamed, as if delighted with the thought.

Daniel was unaccountably touched, even knowing that Lige was at the age to have completely different plans tomorrow. "I'll save a place for you," he said. He frowned, lifting his head. "I thought I heard a car, but I guess not. Here, can you put this on the floor?" He handed down a cabinet door, gripping it until he was sure Lige could manage.

Funny. He thought he heard something again, but it must be Rebecca in the storeroom. Once or twice, he'd heard her humming, so she must be feeling happy. Well, why not? She was getting what she wanted. And it was all she wanted.

He was climbing down the ladder when he heard something again, and this time there was no doubt what it was. A baby was crying in the shop. Someone had come in, and apparently neither they nor Rebecca had realized it.

Since he was near the door, he stepped through it, intent on telling the customer that Rebecca would be right in. But there wasn't a customer. Just the sound of crying coming from the cradle he'd refurbished, and tiny hands waved in the air, setting it swaying.

Daniel covered the floor in a few long strides, reached the cradle and came to an abrupt halt. He wasn't imagining things. There was a baby in the cradle—a girl, to judge by the pink bonnet and the blanket she'd kicked off. Apparently she didn't want to be there, because she was crying lustily, and her small face was bright red.

"Daniel, what…" Rebecca's footsteps sounded as she crossed the floor quickly behind him.

"It's a baby," he said, knowing he sounded idiotic.

"Obviously it's a baby." Rebecca bent over the cradle and picked up the squalling bundle. "Hush, now, hush. Everything will be all right."

Holding the baby close against her, she patted it. Apparently that was the right thing to do. After a few more cries, the infant snuggled against her shoulder.

"Where's the mother?" Daniel pointed out the thing that was far more shocking than a baby in a display cradle. He looked around, but the shop was empty except for them and Lige, who was staring, his eyes huge. And the baby. "We don't even know whose she is."

"Don't be silly," Rebecca said. "I know perfectly well whose she is. This is little Betsy, Shannon's baby. You know, the young Englisch woman from the quilting circle."

Daniel tried to focus, amazed that Rebecca was taking this so easily. He vaguely remembered the young woman. Mary Ann had been walking around with a baby during the quilting group—this baby, he supposed.

"I'm glad you know that much. But what is she doing here without her mammi?"

Rebecca glanced out the front window. "Maybe Shannon went back to her car for something."

Sounded reasonable, but he didn't think so. He walked out onto the porch, looked around and came back in, a bad feeling settling in the pit of his stomach.

"She's not out there, Rebecca. It looks as if she put her baby in the cradle and then just…left." His mind grappled with the problem that presented.

"There has to be a reason." Again, Rebecca sounded perfectly calm in these extraordinary circumstances. "Look in the cradle. Is there anything else?"

He stooped, moving a couple of baby quilts out of the way. "A diaper bag." He hefted it. "Filled up with stuff, by the weight of it. And there's a note." He picked up the folded paper, started to open it and then realized that it was marked with Rebecca's name. He handed it to her, watching her with a worried frown.

Rebecca flipped the paper open and began to read, her brows drawing together. "Shannon doesn't say much. 'Please watch Betsy for me. I can't do it. I can't manage…' It just trails off then." She shook her head. "Poor thing."

He wasn't sure if she was referring to the mother or the baby. "Rebecca, you must call the police. This is for them to handle."

Rebecca stared at him. "Call the police? For what? Shannon asked me to watch the baby for her. People don't call the police for that."

"She didn't exactly ask you. She left the baby with a note. People might say she deserted her baby."

"No one will say that unless the police are called."

Rebecca sounded as if she knew exactly what she was going to do. "That poor girl was alone most of the time with a young baby and no one to help her. She was just overwhelmed, that's all. Every young mother feels that way sometimes."

"But…"

"No buts about it. I'm not going to report her for feeling the way plenty of perfectly fine mothers do. They might take her baby away if I did that. I'm going to do just as she asked and watch Betsy for her."

"Rebecca, stop and think." He couldn't help being afraid for her. "Maybe lots of mammis feel that way, but most of them don't run away."

"I know." For an instant, worry darkened her eyes, and then she looked at the infant in her arms and cradled it close to her. "I understand what you're saying, Daniel. But try to understand how I feel. Shannon felt desperate, with no one to help her. As soon as she comes to her senses, she'll return. I have to give her that chance."

He opened his mouth to protest again, saw that it wasn't going to do any good and closed it again. He looked at the child and saw trouble. But obviously Rebecca looked at her and saw a baby to love and a mother to help.

The little one started to fuss again, chewing on her fist this time.

"I think she wants something to eat," Lige said.

"I think you're right." Rebecca smiled at him. "I'd better warm up a bottle for her. Here." Without warning, she plopped the baby into Daniel's arms, and they automatically curved to receive her. "You amuse her while I do that."

"I'm no good with a boppli," he protested. "Maybe you should call Leah…"

"Don't be silly." She was already nearly out of the room. "Just bounce her a little." She disappeared into the kitchen with the diaper bag.

Left alone, he looked helplessly at Lige, as if a six-year-old would be able to rescue him.

"You could sit in the rocking chair and rock her," Lige said. "That's what Mammi does when I'm sick. And I can talk to her. I like babies."

Since he didn't have a plan of his own, that sounded reasonable. Balancing the child carefully, he went to the rocking chair and sat, holding her against his body the way Rebecca had. Lige leaned over the arm of the chair and made cooing sounds.

Apparently that worked, because she stopped fussing. Her arms waved as if she tried to reach Lige's face.

Daniel was glad little Betsy was happy, but he certain sure wasn't happy himself. He didn't know where this situation would end, but he didn't like the idea of Rebecca getting involved. Why had the Englisch woman picked her?

The answer was obvious when he put it like that. She'd picked Rebecca because Rebecca was kind, gentle and loving. He just hoped those qualities weren't going to land her in a peck of trouble.

Rebecca dwelled on what Daniel had said while she warmed the bottle in a pan on the stove. Daniel wanted what was best for her of course. She didn't doubt that. She knew he feared her getting entangled with the Englisch world in a way that might hurt her.

But he didn't know Shannon, and he probably couldn't understand what she and Leah had seen instantly about the young woman—the loneliness and the sense of being overwhelmed. And how she'd changed when she'd felt the understanding and acceptance of the women in the quilting group. It had been like watching a flower opening.

Only another mother could understand how complicated a woman's feelings were with a first child. Surely every mother had, at some time or other, feared that she was a terrible mother, that she couldn't do this, that, if she couldn't relax for a few minutes, she'd fly apart. They'd talked about it the day of the quilting group.

Guilt nibbled at Rebecca's heart as she tested the bottle. She'd understood, but she hadn't done anything. Caught up in her own problems, she'd ignored a neighbor in need. She could have stopped in town to check on Shannon one day, but she hadn't. All the more reason why she had to do what she could now.

Shannon would be back. She was perfectly sure of that. Probably, as soon as she'd managed to get some rest, she'd wake up, realize what she'd done and return. How could Rebecca possibly run the risk that Shannon would find herself in the police's hands when she did come back?

Rebecca stood for a moment, the bottle in her hand, a prey to apprehension. No matter what she'd said to Daniel, she had to admit that she was a little afraid of what tomorrow would bring.

A saying of her grandmother's slipped into her mind so clearly that Grossmammi might be standing there beside her. *Don't worry about tomorrow. Just*

*do what God puts in front of you right now and leave
the rest to Him.*

Grossmammi had been a wise woman, and Rebecca
would do her best to follow that advice. Carrying the
bottle, she went through the door to the shop. There
she stopped, her heart seized by the sight before her.

Daniel sat in the rocking chair, cuddling the baby.
He was crooning to her in Pennsylvania Dutch, his
voice soft and soothing, while Lige hung on the arm
of the rocker, totally entranced.

Oh, Daniel. Watching him made her heart ache. He
deserved to have a wife who loved him and children
to love. If only he could get past his conviction that he
was to blame for the decisions other people had made.

He glanced up and saw her, giving her a smile. "It's
working. She's stopped crying."

"She'll be even happier once her little tummy is
full." Coming to them, she handed him the bottle.

"Wait—shouldn't you do this? What if I get it
wrong?"

The panicked look on his face made her laugh.
"There's no wrong about it. Just put the nipple in her
mouth. She'll know what to do with it."

Sure enough, Betsy was already waving her hands
toward the bottle, trying to grab it. Daniel barely got
the nipple within reach of her mouth when she was
sucking noisily, her face pink with effort.

"She really likes it, doesn't she?" Lige hung over
her in fascination. "She likes us, too. Can we keep
her, Mammi?"

"No, no, we can't keep her. She's not ours." She
was going to explain further, but Lige wasn't finished.

"She could be ours," he insisted. "You could be the

mammi, and Daniel could be the daadi, and I could be the big bruder. I'd be a gut big bruder."

Rebecca couldn't look at Daniel, and she knew her cheeks were as pink as the baby's. "I'm sure you'd be a fine big bruder, Lige. But Betsy is Shannon's baby. She's a lady in my quilting group. We're just baby-sitting her for a while."

She wished she could say how long, but she couldn't.

The sound of a horse's hooves and buggy wheels drew Rebecca's attention to the front window, and she watched in dismay as Lydia Schultz climbed down. She glanced at Daniel, but he was totally occupied with the baby.

She could hardly ask him to go and hide with the baby. Somehow, she'd just have to handle Lydia's nosi-ness for herself.

Lydia came in, and of course her eyes went in-stantly to Daniel and the baby. Then they shifted to Rebecca, and she saw too clearly the rampant curios-ity raging in them.

"I didn't know you had an infant, Rebecca."

She certain sure knew Rebecca didn't have any such thing, but it wouldn't help to point that out. Re-becca tried to produce a natural-sounding laugh.

"Lige is wishing I did," she said. "No, I'm just watching her for a friend. What can I help you with today, Lydia?" She took an inviting step toward the fabrics, but Lydia didn't follow the hint.

"It looks like Daniel is the one who's babysitting, ain't so?" Her head poked toward Daniel with the question.

Rebecca remembered Sam saying that the reason

Lydia's nose was so pointed was because she kept poking it into other people's business. That had earned him a reproof from Leah, but Leah thought it true nonetheless.

"I had my hands full for a moment, so Daniel stepped in," she said. "Lige, would you go and see if your cousin Mary Ann or Aunt Leah can help me for a bit? We should let Daniel get back to his own work."

Lige tore himself away from the baby and spurted out the back door. Daniel probably wished he could go with him. But he was smiling pleasantly at Lydia.

"Go on and take care of whatever Lydia needs," he said, giving Lydia a bland smile. "The cabinets will wait a few more minutes."

"Denke," she murmured, grateful that he was taking it so well. She turned back to Lydia again. "What was it you said you needed?"

Maybe sensing there was no more to be gained from Daniel, Lydia moved toward the rows of fabric bolts. "I need some backing material, but I haven't decided what color yet. I brought some samples from the pieced top."

Rebecca nodded, taking in the color scheme of the swatches Lydia held. "Something in the yellow or rust colors, maybe?" She led the way to the solid colors.

"Whose baby did you say that was?" Lydia was obviously not done probing.

"An Englisch friend of mine," she said and tried to emulate Daniel's cool smile. She pulled out a few bolts of suitable colors. "Perhaps one of these would do."

Maybe the smile worked, because Lydia got down to business and concentrated on the fabrics. Of course, she still wasn't easy to please. She had to pull every bolt out twice, at least, before she decided what she wanted, and she had one bolt carried to the cutting table before deciding on a different one.

Finally she was gone, but before Rebecca could say anything to Daniel, she heard Lige coming back. It sounded as if he had both Leah and Mary Ann with him, and they all came into the shop together.

Mary Ann headed straight for the baby. "I'll take her, Daniel. Did you burp her yet?"

He shook his head. "Nobody's taught me burping." He grinned at her. "I'm sure you're just fine at it." He rose, smiling down at the little one in his arms before transferring her carefully to Mary Ann. "Goodbye for now, little one. Lige, I guess we're not needed here, so we'll get back to work."

Once they'd gone, Leah caught Rebecca's arm and drew her a little away. "How did you get Daniel to do that? I've never seen him with a baby before."

"I just plopped her in his arms. He had to either take her or drop her." She smiled, remembering his tenderness with the baby. "He got to like it once he did."

Leah nodded, smiling. "He needs a family, that's certain sure. But what about Shannon?"

"I didn't see her. If I had, maybe I could have helped." She drew out the note Shannon had left and gave it to Leah, who read it quickly.

"Ach, poor child. I don't know which one I feel worse for, but the boppli won't remember anything of it. Poor Shannon. She came right out and said how lonely she was. Why didn't I go to see her?"

"That's just what I feel myself." It relieved her considerably to hear Leah echo her own thoughts. "Daniel thought at first I should go to the police, but I can't do that. Think what it would do to that little family."

Leah considered it, her face solemn. "Yah, I see. No, we can't go to the police. Not unless she doesn't come back in a few days."

"She will," Rebecca said, squashing any doubts she might have. "She'll come to herself and realize what she's done. You know how it is with a first baby, and her without any family or friends to help her, and her husband away, as well."

"Taking care of the boppli is no problem," Leah said. "We'll all help, and be glad of a chance to do something gut for the young woman. Beyond that, it's in the hands of the gut Lord."

Rebecca nodded, sending up a silent prayer for Shannon, wherever she was. Perhaps she'd call her husband, and he'd be able to help.

"That's all we can do." Rebecca smiled at the sight of Mary Ann in the rocking chair with the baby, but her wayward imagination kept showing her an image of Daniel sitting there, cradling the infant.

Lige's innocent words came back to her, and she could feel herself blushing just thinking of it. She'd have to say something to Daniel—something light, just making a joke of it. But she couldn't think how she was going to manage it.

Chapter Twelve

Rebecca had forgotten what it was like to be roused from sleep by the cry of a hungry baby. By the time she'd warmed the bottle, it seemed forever, until Betsy was contentedly sucking away.

Rebecca settled back in a comfortable position against the headboard of the bed. As far as she could tell, Lige hadn't stirred from his bed in the next room, and she hadn't roused anyone else.

No, she'd been wrong, she realized as the door opened softly. Mamm slipped in. Rebecca smiled at her. With her graying blond hair in the loose plaits she wore at night, Mamm looked even younger than she did normally, her face round and rosy with sleep.

She came and settled down on the bed, reaching across to give the baby a pat.

"Betsy woke you," Rebecca said softly. "I'm sorry."

Mamm just smiled. "No mother ever loses her re-action to a baby's cry." She studied Betsy for a moment. "She'll be giving up that middle-of-the-night feed soon, I'd think. Lige had by this age, ain't so?"

"Mostly," Rebecca said. "But if he did wake, it

certain sure was easier, since I wasn't fooling with bottles."

"Maybe the strange place troubled her, poor little mite," Mamm said. "Think how upset her mammi must have been to leave her here."

Rebecca had thought of little else. "I guess we were the first people who took an interest in Shannon since she moved here. It sounded as if she'd been holed up in her house, alone with the baby, except for coming to quilting."

Mamm nodded. "It's not easy to make friends in a new place, I guess. Still, most folks are kind, if you give them a chance."

"I had a chance to do more, and I didn't." Her guilt pushed the words out. "I knew she was lonely and overwhelmed. I could have gone to see her."

"So could any of us," Mamm said. "We get caught up in our own lives and don't see our neighbor in need. This will be a gut lesson for us, I think."

Both Leah and Mamm had expressed the same guilt she felt. That didn't make it less, but as Mamm said, God was teaching them a lesson they needed.

"She reminds me of when Lige was this size. Hard to believe that now, when he's starting to outgrow my lap." She stroked the fuzz of fine hair on the baby's head.

"The years slip away fast," Mamm said. "The boppli becomes a child, then a girl, then a woman with a family of her own, all in the twinkling of an eye." She was silent for a moment, maybe remembering the time when her own young ones were babies. "It's wonderful gut to have you back here, my Rebecca. Mind, I love Leah like a daughter, but still, it's not the same. A woman wants the comfort of a daughter nearby as she gets old."

"You're not old," Rebecca protested.

"Maybe, but it's a different stage of life when it's your grandchildren clustered around instead of your kinder. Having you and Lige here is such a blessing I hadn't expected ever to have."

Rebecca looked down at the baby in her arms, wishing... What? She couldn't change what she'd already done, and at least she had Lige. He was worth any hardship she had to endure. And even though there had been times when God had been silent, she'd always known He was holding her up.

"It means so much for me to be here. Just to know that my home was here, waiting for me, after..." She let that trail off, not wanting to get into the subject of her marriage.

Her mother leaned toward her, her face filled with love and pain. "Ach, Rebecca, you don't need to tell me anything. I already guessed a lot about your marriage to James, and what we didn't guess, his daad told yours."

"He did?" She'd thought she was finished being surprised by the Mast family. "I never thought he would say anything."

They'd always tried to protect James. She'd understood that, but it hadn't really helped any of them.

"It's in the past now." Mamm patted her. "Hard as it is to forget, you must forgive."

"I have," she protested. "At least, I've tried. I want so much to just...get on with our lives, mine and Lige's."

"Yah, I know." She smiled a little. "Lige says he wants a baby sister or bruder."

"I know." She didn't want to talk about something that was so unlikely, nor to try to explain why she felt that way.

"Rebecca." Her mother's voice was serious, and she reached toward Rebecca as if she had something important to say. "What happened with James doesn't mean that you must live alone the rest of your life. Surely God will give you a man to love in your future, a good man who is all the things James wasn't."

Rebecca was swept by the longing to express her doubts and fears. She tried to suppress it. "I…I can't. I can't risk it. How can I trust myself and Lige to someone else?"

"Ach, Rebecca, you were eighteen when you met James and fell in love. You only knew him for a month before you decided to marry him."

True enough. "I was young and foolish."

"You're not young and foolish now," Mamm pointed out. "You're home, surrounded by people you've known all your life. You can take time and let love and trust grow." Before Rebecca could protest, Mamm stood up. "I won't push. Just think on it," she said. "Good night."

The door closed behind her before Rebecca could find a response. Betsy lolled in her arms, limp and drowsy. As she tended to the baby and tucked her up in the crib Sam had moved into the room, Rebecca searched her heart for an answer.

Had Mamm been thinking of Daniel? True, he wasn't far from her own thoughts these days. Strange, that just when she was thinking it might someday be possible for her to love him, that Daniel, in his pre-occupation with his brother, should seem to move further away from her.

Daniel, packing up what he'd need for the day of work, looked up when the workshop door opened.

"Onkel Zeb. What brings you out here? Is there something Caleb wants me to do?"

"No, no, only to get on with your own work." Zeb glanced over the contents of the workbench. "You're going over to Rebecca's place, ain't so?"

He nodded. "I'd like to finish the prep work in the kitchen. She'll need to have the electric refrigerator taken out, so I'd like everything ready for the new one."

"Gut." He spoke absently, and Daniel realized something was on his mind—something other than the work Daniel proposed to do that day.

"So, what is it?" Daniel snapped his toolbox closed. "I can tell when you're deciding whether or not to speak, you know."

His uncle smiled, but his faded blue eyes were grave. "Guess I'd better just spit it out, ain't so? When I was in town, I heard rumors. Gossip, that is."

"About what?" Zeb's seriousness alarmed him. "Something about Aaron?"

"Ach, no. Not Aaron. It was about Rebecca, and the baby that's turned up at her place all of a sudden." He met Daniel's gaze. "And about you being involved somehow."

"Lydia." He clenched his fists on the edge of the workbench. "I know it."

"Lydia?" Onkel Zeb looked confused, as well he might. "Is that the name of the boppli?"

"Lydia Schultz. The little one's name is Betsy." Seeing that Onkel Zeb looked confused, he went on, choosing his words. "You know what a blabbermaul Lydia is. She came in the quilt shop yesterday and saw me holding the baby. Of course she'd have to make a big story of it."

Zeb shook his head, but at least he was smiling now. "Whose baby?"

"Rebecca is watching the daughter of an Englisch friend of hers while the woman's away. You know what a kind person she is. She'd never say no when someone needs her."

"So that's it. Leave it to Lydia to make a big story out of something simple."

"That's certain sure."

He was relieved that his uncle accepted it so easily, but he reminded himself he wasn't out of the woods with this story. He'd have to tell Rebecca what was going on. She'd be upset, but it would be worse if she heard it from someone else.

"I'd best be on my way." He clapped his uncle on the shoulder. "Denke. I'd rather hear it now than have folks talking and not know it."

"I think I'll make an excuse for another trip to the hardware store," Zeb said. "That'll give me a chance to set the story straight." He grinned, as if he looked forward to it. He always said the men did as much gossiping in the hardware store as the women did anywhere else.

Raising his hand in farewell, Daniel strode out of

the workshop and off toward Rebecca's place. The sooner she knew what was going on, the better.

Maybe he should speak to her again about talking to the police. How long was she willing to wait for Shannon to come back? This couldn't go on for long, especially with people already talking.

All was quiet when he went in the back door of the shop. Maybe she had left the baby back at the farmhouse, out of sight of any customers. Or maybe Shannon had returned.

But when he pushed open the door, he realized he'd been wrong on both counts. Rebecca sat in the rocking chair, moving slowly forward and backward, the baby in her arms. A tiny hand waved, brushing her cheek, and she kissed it lightly.

Daniel couldn't move. All he could do was stand and stare at her, while his imagination gave him a picture of Rebecca looking lovingly at their baby. He could see it, could even imagine what their boppli would look like, with Rebecca's clear blue eyes and a little fluff of blond hair on its head.

No. The reaction hit him hard. He couldn't let himself think that way. Bad enough when he'd entertained those thoughts about Rebecca and Lige, but what about other children they might have if he let himself love her? How could he let them rely on him, when he'd already failed the two people he'd loved most?

Even as he thought he'd back out without disturbing her, Rebecca looked up and saw him. She smiled, and that sweet smile nearly did him in.

"It's all right," she said. "I'm not trying to put her to sleep. Just enjoying her company until Mary Ann gets here to watch her. Komm. I know Betsy would like to see you."

Daniel walked toward her, struggling to compose himself. "I don't think Betsy even knows who I am." But he bent over her obediently, unable to resist smiling when the baby's eyes focused on his face. "How are you this morning? Did you keep everyone up?"

"Not at all. Well, she did get me up for one feeding in the night, and Mamm came in and kept me company, but Lige and Daadi slept right through it."

"They would." He grinned. "I probably would, too." He'd have his chance to find out when Caleb and Jessie's baby was right there in the room across the hall from him.

"Mammi says that a mother never loses the ability to wake up at the cry of a baby." She smiled down at the little one. "I hated to disturb her sleep, but it was gut to sit and talk in the quiet."

Was he imagining it, or did Rebecca's cheeks flush slightly when she said the words? It made him wonder what women talked about in the middle of the night.

Much as he hated to upset the peace between them, he had to ask the question that was in his mind. "Have you heard anything from the baby's mother?"

"Not yet. But soon, I'm sure." There might be the faintest trace of doubt in her voice.

"Maybe…"

"No," she said. "I know what you're thinking, but I'm not going to go to the police and say that Shannon deserted her baby."

"You wouldn't have to say it that way," he protested. "After all, you might be worried about her safety, since you haven't heard from her. It would be logical to ask the police for help in case she's sick or had an accident."

"And how would I answer all the questions they'd be sure to ask me?" She shook her head. "I can't. I know you mean well, Daniel, but I just can't."

He'd argue, but he knew it wouldn't do any good. Besides, the door opened and Lige rushed in, followed more quietly by Mary Ann.

"Daniel. Did you see the baby? What's she doing?"

"Nothing much." He grinned as he watched Lige lean over her, staring in fascination. "Babies that age don't do much."

But Lige wasn't paying attention. He tugged at his mother's sleeve. "Mary Ann says I can help her watch Betsy. Can I, Mammi?"

Rebecca glanced from his face to Daniel. "I thought you were going to help Daniel today."

"Oh." Lige stared at him in consternation. "I forgot."

"It's all right," Daniel said, giving in to the obviously strong attraction of the baby. "Why don't you babysit until the little one falls asleep and then come help me?"

Lige nodded eagerly. "All right, Mammi?"

Rebecca seemed silently to consult with Mary Ann before she nodded. "Be sure you listen to Mary Ann, though."

"I will."

Rebecca stood, shifting the baby to Mary Ann's arms, and Lige bounced along beside his cousin as they headed out the back.

In a way, it was a relief to Daniel when they'd gone. Somehow he had to bring up the subject of the gossip Onkel Zeb had heard, and he was afraid it would hurt her.

Maybe the only way was to just come out with it.

"There is something I must talk with you about, Rebecca."

Her gaze was slightly impatient. "I thought we'd already discussed the impossibility of talking to the police."

"We have. I'm not sure I agree with you, but I respect your right to make that decision. You must know that, Rebecca."

"I'm sorry." Her expression was rueful. "I wish I weren't in this position, but I am, so I must make the best of it."

He couldn't expect that Rebecca's loving heart would allow her to follow any other path. In fact, he wouldn't want her to. Did she even realize how much she'd changed since she'd come home? He suspected she was becoming the woman she'd have been if she hadn't ever met James.

"Onkel Zeb was at the hardware store when he heard something that troubled him." He paused, trying to come up with the right words, and then pushed on. "He says there's some mixed-up gossip going around about you and the baby. He came to me about it, because apparently my name figured into it."

They looked at each other, and he could see the understanding dawn in her face. "Lydia," she said.

"I'm certain sure that's the source. Who else could it be?" He shook his head. "I'm trying hard not to judge a sister in the church, but it's not easy. I hope... well, that you're not too upset by it."

Rebecca had the air of one picking up a burden. "I can't say I'm surprised. Especially since…"

"What? Is there some reason Lydia would do such a thing?" It seemed important to him to get to the bottom of it. Surely Rebecca, after all her griefs, shouldn't have to put up with gossip in her own community.

"Lydia has a cousin in the area where we lived in Ohio." Rebecca seemed to study the display of quilt bindings on the rack next to her. "When everything was going on with James, I'm afraid there was a lot of talk. Some folks thought it was disloyal of me to go to the bishop about him."

"That's ridiculous." The very idea made him hot with protective anger. "James was not a well man. Surely the Leit could understand that you were trying to help him. Especially when the bishop himself intervened."

"Most people did, I think." She pressed her fingers against her temples, as if her head had begun to ache. "But there were those who questioned."

It didn't take all that much imagination to see the reasons. "If he had had a broken leg or a heart condition, they'd understand that you had to push him to see the right doctors to help him."

"Exactly." Rebecca gave him a quick glance, but it was long enough for him to see the way memory darkened her eyes. "It was his brain that was hurt, and that's harder for anyone to understand. Maybe that made it more natural for folks to question and wonder."

"So you think Lydia heard some of this from her cousin." He could see that easily. Cousins stayed in touch, and most likely, there were regular letters exchanged.

"If not at first, then certainly when it became known that I was coming here to live. She'd have written, probably rehashing the old rumors." A tiny smile flickered and was gone. "It won't surprise you to hear that Lydia's cousin had her own reputation as a blabbermaul."

"It must run in the family." He dared to touch Rebecca's arm lightly. "I'm sorry for it. I explained to Onkel Zeb that you were watching the baby for an Englisch friend, that's all. Not that he'd believe anything else." He made a disgusted sound. "Anyone with any sense would realize that the baby wasn't yours. How could it be?"

"I don't think sense is a necessary quality for people who like to tell tales." Her tone was mild, and he realized she was getting over the initial shock. "Please tell your uncle that I appreciate his letting me know."

He managed to smile. "Don't think Onkel Zeb is stopping there. He was looking forward to heading right back down to the hardware store and setting folks straight." His initial enjoyment of Zeb's attitude slipped away. "The only thing is that he doesn't know everything. I didn't tell him about Shannon just leaving the baby here without asking."

"No, we can't let that get around." She rubbed her temples again. "I wish I could see what was for the best. If I don't hear from her by tomorrow..."

Daniel struggled to see a path forward that would be best for everyone. "If you're right that she'd come to her senses soon, I'd think surely you would hear by then." He hesitated, not wanting to suggest something that would offend her. "Is there anyone among the Englisch women in the quilting group that you could talk to? Someone you could trust to understand and maybe give you advice?"

Rebecca was silent for so long that he started to think she wouldn't answer. At last she looked at him, her face troubled. "I hate the idea of telling anyone what she's done. But there is someone who might understand."

"Who?" He'd give a lot to have this burden lifted from Rebecca. Or at least to have someone to share it.

"There's Glenda Allen. She's the older woman that Mamm knows. She seemed to have sympathy for Shannon, and she might understand."

"She'd look at it from an Englisch woman's point of view," he said carefully. "That might be a help."

He could see the struggle going on in Rebecca's heart. Finally she nodded. "If I haven't heard from Shannon by the time the quilters come tomorrow, I'll think about telling Glenda the whole thing. I just hope I'm not making a mistake."

Everything in him yearned to reassure her, even to take the burden from her shoulders. Her eyes met his, and it seemed she knew exactly what he was thinking.

"I don't think you can make a mistake when you're acting out of love." Daniel lifted his hand to touch the soft curve of her cheek. It felt like down under his fingertips, and warmth spread through him, making his skin tingle. Even that light touch was enough to make him long for more.

Rebecca didn't draw away from his touch, and her eyes darkened as they met his gaze. Her lips parted on an indrawn breath. For an instant, he couldn't breathe. They were so close. A step would bring her into his arms.

And then he remembered all the reasons why he couldn't do this. He couldn't risk hurting her. She was too precious for that. But stepping away from the hope in her face was the hardest thing he'd ever done.

Chapter Thirteen

Rebecca felt the day dragging on and tried to dismiss Daniel from her thoughts. She couldn't change him. Only God could do that, and even their loving God could act only if Daniel made himself open to realizing what he was doing to himself.

Those moments when he had touched her face came surging into her thoughts too frequently to be ignored. She put her palm against her cheek. It seemed to be still warm from his hand. They'd looked at each other, and she'd seen the barriers between them crumble. She was a different person now from the frightened, embittered woman she'd been such a short time ago. In another moment, they would have kissed. But Daniel… Daniel had drawn away.

Rebecca found herself looking up at every sound, hoping and praying that it would be Shannon. But although several cars pulled in, none of them contained the person she wanted to see.

And invariably, after each customer had left and the shop was quiet, her thoughts returned to Daniel.

"I am being wonderful foolish, ain't so, little one?"

She smiled down at Betsy, ensconced in a basket Leah had brought over.

Betsy waved her arms as if in agreement. Then she seemed to lose interest, having caught sight of her foot in the air. She became engrossed in trying to catch it with her hands and, once she succeeded, brought it to her mouth.

Rebecca couldn't help but laugh. "Now, that's a big accomplishment, Betsy."

The back door swung open. "Did you say something, Rebecca?" Daniel stood in the doorway.

Praying he hadn't heard all of it, she managed to smile in what she hoped was a normal way. "I was just talking to the baby. I sent Mary Ann and Lige back to the house to have their lunch."

He took a couple of steps forward and then stopped, as if determined to leave a good big space between them. For safety's sake, she supposed.

"I wanted to tell you that I'll have to be away for a couple of days later in the week or maybe over the weekend."

Was he so panic-stricken at what had nearly happened between them that he felt the need to run away from her?

"I see. That's fine." She wanted to ask where he was going, but she couldn't.

Daniel stood for a moment, irresolute, and she could see him struggle to say something. If he intended to talk about what had happened between them, she'd be mortified.

"You know that letter I said I was going to write to Aaron?"

Her thoughts had been so occupied by what was

happening between them that it took Rebecca a moment to refocus. "What about it? Did you write it?"

He made a rueful face. "I wrote it about ten times before I gave up. I couldn't find the right words, not in a letter."

"I'm sorry." It was all she could find to say. What a pity if he gave up so quickly on approaching Aaron. But perhaps it was for the best. Who was she to judge?

"So I've decided. I'm going to see him." He sounded determined.

She stared at Daniel's face, hardly able to believe the words. No such thought had been in his head when they'd talked about Aaron. She'd have known, if so.

"Are you sure that's the right thing to do?"

It would be hurtful enough if he wrote a letter at her suggestion and then Aaron didn't answer. How much worse would it be if he saw Aaron in person and Aaron rejected him? Was she setting him up for more pain? She should have stayed out of it.

"Yah, I'm sure. I feel it. Don't worry." He smiled at her, seeming to look right into her scrambled thoughts. "This is my decision, just like coming home is Aaron's. If I end up getting hurt, it's still better than not seeing him and telling him we still love and want him."

His words stilled any objection she might have made. "I understand. I'll be praying for you and for Aaron. When do you leave?"

"Not until after this business with the baby is settled. I couldn't go before then. I've made arrangements with Dave Smith to drive me, and we'll go out one day. I'll see Aaron, and we'll come back the next. He doesn't mind all the driving, and I don't want to be away longer than that."

"If it's better for you to go now, you should do it."
She tried not to show how bereft she'd feel if he took
her up on that. "You don't need to stay here for my
benefit, and there's really nothing anyone can do."

"No." He looked a little disconcerted at her words.
"I suppose not, but still, I'll feel better if I'm around.
Just in case you need me." He forced a smile. "After
all, I was the one who found Betsy first, remember?"

"Only by a hair," she responded, smiling a little.

But she didn't press the idea, because if she were
honest with herself, she wanted him here. She had
family supporting her, but as Daniel said, he'd been
in on this from the beginning. And Daniel...well, he
was Daniel, her rock.

He was frowning a little as he watched the baby.
"Are you still thinking you'll talk to your mamm's
friend about Shannon and the baby if she's not back
tomorrow?"

Rebecca nodded. "I'll ask her to come a little early
so we can talk privately. I feel as if I know her better than the others, and Mamm thinks highly of her."

"You're worried," he said, taking a step closer.

"For sure. I've been worried from the beginning. If
only Shannon would come back on her own. I wish I
knew how to get in touch with her husband."

"Surely she wouldn't let him return from his trip
and find her gone." But Daniel's tone said he could
imagine that too easily. After all, it was what his own
mother had done.

There was nothing she could say about that, clearly.
"Glenda may have some idea about how to reach him.
Or even a cell phone number for Shannon." She looked
down at the baby, deeply engrossed in sucking on

her foot. "I can't believe she won't come back by tomorrow."

"I pray you're right." He hesitated. "Whether she does or not, I won't be leaving as long as you might need me. That's what friends are for, ain't so?"

She forced herself to nod, to smile. And to pretend that her heart wasn't aching. Daniel was her friend, and he'd made it clear that was all he'd ever be.

Glenda came early the next afternoon, as Rebecca had asked. By that time, Rebecca's nerves were stretched to the limit, and the questions kept ricocheting around in her mind. Was she doing the right thing? What if something had happened to Shannon? What if she didn't come back?

In fact, she was so shaken she no longer had any doubts about sharing the burden. She had to confide in Glenda. So she poured out the whole story, holding Betsy in her arms and bouncing her gently to comfort her.

"Did I do the right thing? What should I do now?" She didn't intend to sound quite so panicky, but that was how she felt.

The lines around Glenda's eyes and mouth had deepened as she listened, but she immediately reached out to pat Rebecca's shoulder. "I don't see how you could do anything else," she said. "After all, Shannon did ask you to watch the baby, so it's not as if she'd abandoned her."

"But she hasn't been in touch. I thought surely I'd hear something by today." But her tension had eased at the reassuring words.

Glenda nodded slowly, her eyes on the baby. "Betsy is doing all right?"

"She's fine." Rebecca smiled down at her and touched the baby's rosy cheek. "At her age, she doesn't know what's going on, poor little mite."

Glenda was smiling, too. "Shannon knew what she was about when she picked you to care for her baby. Now…if only I had got a cell phone number for her." She shook her head, frustrated. "I have her house phone number, but that won't do us any good."

"Do you know where she lives?" It was embarrassing that she hadn't even found out that much.

"Yes, I did ask her that. I had thought, at the time, that I'd drop in on her. It was obvious that she was lonely. Then I got busy…but that's no excuse. I should have made it a priority."

"That's what I've been telling myself, too. And Leah and Mamm. We all feel so guilty that we did nothing." Rebecca patted the baby's back, feeling the little body relaxing into slumber. "If we could reach her husband… But I don't know if that's the right thing to do or not."

"He has a right to be told, I suppose, but I wish I had some feel for how he'd react. I wouldn't want to cause trouble between them. And anyway, I have no idea how to contact him." Glenda frowned, as if scouring her mind for an answer. "There might be something in her house that would tell us, but that would mean bringing the police into it. I wouldn't want to do that unless I had to."

"Yah, that's what I am thinking, too."

They looked at each other, and it wondered Rebecca

how much risk they were taking by doing nothing. Was that what Glenda feared, too?

Finally Glenda shook her head. "I keep coming back to the thought that Shannon asked you to watch the baby. She must have been overwhelmed even to think of going away, but she behaved responsibly in that, packing the diaper bag and providing the bottles and formula. Still, if we don't hear from her today, we may have to ask for help to find her."

Leah and Mamm came through from the kitchen with Jessie, and Mamm glanced from Rebecca to Glenda. "You have told her then."

She nodded, and Glenda smiled. "I should have known you two would be involved in this. Don't worry too much. We'll sort it out together."

A car pulled up just then. Rebecca's heart leaped, but it was just the other women arriving for quilting.

Another problem loomed in Rebecca's mind. "What should I say to them? I don't know if it's wise to tell anyone else."

Glenda considered. "I think you could trust them. But maybe it's best to keep it between us. Let's just say you're watching the baby for Shannon. I guess there's no need to bring others into it unless we have to."

Rebecca was so relieved to hear her say "we" that she could actually feel her heart lighten. She bent over the cradle, laying Betsy down and pushing it lightly with her knee to make it swing.

Alice and Debby came in, their chattering lowered when they saw the baby. Debby dropped her workbag and came to bend over the cradle. "What a little sweetheart! They grow so fast at that age."

Alice followed her, smiling almost involuntarily at

the sight of the baby. She glanced around. "Where's her mother?"

"Shannon had to be away today," Glenda said before Rebecca could speak. "Rebecca is babysitting."

"What fun." Debby shook her head. "What am I saying? If I spent any amount of time around a little one that age, I'd start wanting another baby myself, just when I've got mine in school all day."

"I loved it when my children were still at home." Alice was just a bit disapproving, which didn't seem to bother Debby in the least.

"That's because you don't remember how wonderful it is to have several hours to yourself." Debby grinned, taking any sting out of the words.

From what Rebecca could see, these two knew each other well despite the obvious difference in their ages. Debby seemed to treat the older woman more like a big sister than anything else.

Debby must have seen her watching them, because she laughed. "Don't worry, Rebecca. Alice doesn't mind me. Despite her attitude, when my kids were babies, she used to come to my house when I was feeling overwhelmed and chase me out for an hour or two. She always said I'd be a better mother if I had some time to myself."

"Nonsense," Alice said, but her cheeks flushed and Rebecca could see the affection in her eyes. Maybe it wouldn't be a bad thing to confide in them.

A car pulled up outside with a shriek of brakes, gravel scattering. For an instant, Rebecca's heart nearly stopped, and then she saw—it was Shannon.

Breathing a silent prayer of thanksgiving that God

had heard her pleas, she hurried to open the door. Shannon rushed in, her face white, her eyes huge.

"My baby—"

Smiling, even as she blinked back tears, Rebecca gestured to the cradle. Shannon flew to it, dropping on her knees as she scooped the baby up in her arms.

"I'm here. Mommy's here. I love you…" The words came out in a rush of sound. "You're all right."

"Of course she's all right," Glenda said. She knelt next to Shannon and put her arms around both of them. "Rebecca was taking care of her."

Galvanized by her response, Rebecca joined them, putting a comforting arm around Shannon's shoulders. "Everything's fine now. You're here, and it's all right."

Shannon looked up, tears staining her cheeks. "I was so ashamed. I just drove and drove until I was so tired I couldn't keep going. I pulled into a park and just fell asleep in my car. When I woke up, I realized what I'd done…how long I'd been gone."

"Komm, now." Rebecca patted her. "You did exactly what I thought. As soon as you had some sleep, you came back. I knew you would."

From the corner of her eye, she saw Alice open her mouth, but a look from Glenda silenced her.

"It seemed to take forever to come back. I ran out of gas, and I was frantic by the time someone stopped and helped me. I thought I'd never get here, and all I could do was pray." She stroked the baby's head and showered it with kisses. "How could I have done such a thing? I'm not fit to be a mother."

"Now, stop that. You were all alone, and you most likely have postpartum depression, as well." Alice came closer, touching Shannon gently. "I did. It was so bad I can't talk about it even now. But I got help, and you will, too."

Rebecca could only stare at Alice, seeing the tears in her eyes. In spite of the things she'd said, she did understand. More, she did something about it.

"That's right," Debby said. "You just need to have family to help you. Since they're far away, we'll fill in. We'll be your family." She joined them, so that they were surrounding Shannon and the baby, touching each other, united.

Surrounded by love, Rebecca thought, her heart full. They were good people, and they knew what it was to be a new mother. They wouldn't let Shannon down. Shannon would have their help for as long as she needed it, and one day she might have a chance to help another young mother, and she would remember.

Daniel, coming toward the shop, late that afternoon, paused and watched as the women from Rebecca's quilting group came out. They were clustered around the younger woman, Shannon, who held little Betsy close in her arms.

He felt a momentary pang at realizing the baby was leaving. She'd grabbed hold of his heart with her small hand in the time she'd been here. Still, he'd no doubt see her again when the quilting group met.

So things had worked out just as Rebecca hoped. She stood, watching as the cars pulled out one after the other, lifting her hand in a wave. Leah and Mamm headed for the farmhouse, and Jessie started toward home, giving him a quick wave.

He waited for a moment until they'd all got on their

ways. Then he propped the plywood he'd been carrying against the porch railing and went to join her.

"So you were right," he said. "Shannon did come back."

Rebecca turned the full force of her joy on him, and it rocked his heart. "Ach, it was wonderful fine to see. As soon as she came to her senses, she turned around and started back. And the other women—they were so loving with her. They won't let her down."

"No. And you won't either, I'd guess."

"I should have acted before," she said, starting back into the shop and seeming to take it for granted that he would come. "Thank the good Lord I had a second chance."

A second chance. He repeated the words thoughtfully. Was that what he was looking for? A second chance to do the right thing?

They'd reached the shop, and Rebecca stood for a moment, looking at the circle of chairs she'd put out. Her lips curved in amusement. "No one got much quilting done today, I'm afraid. But there will be plenty more chances."

"About Shannon…" He began, thinking there was more to be said.

"She'll be all right. They're all rallying around her. We'll make sure someone goes to see her every day when her husband isn't there."

"Do you think Shannon will tell him? Her husband, I mean?"

Rebecca hesitated. "I don't know. I haven't met him, so how can I tell what kind of man he is? If she can trust him to understand, that would be the best thing for that little family, ain't so?"

"Yah." There it was again. Trust. Each time she mentioned it was like a little dart in his soul.

Bending, Rebecca pulled the sheet from the cradle pad. "I guess you never thought what use the cradle would be put to when you brought it to me." She seemed just a little sad as she rearranged baby quilts on the cradle.

"No, but I'm glad it was here. Glad it could be used the way it was intended." He helped her fold one of the quilts. "You're sorry not to have the baby around, ain't so?"

"I guess I am. But happy for Shannon, for sure." She glanced at him and then looked down again at the yellow and white crib quilt in her hands. "Shannon needed a family desperately and didn't have one. And I…I had a family loving me and longing to help, and I kept trying to push them away."

"Maybe so. But you're different now."

A smile touched her lips again. "Yah, thanks to all of you. I remembered what it feels like to love and trust."

Daniel's heart was so full in that moment that it seemed words would pour from him. He couldn't let it happen. Much as he cared about Rebecca, fear still held him back—fear of himself.

Silence fell between them, and he didn't know how to break it. At last Rebecca did. Giving the quilt a last twitch in place, she turned away from him.

"At least now that things are settled with Shannon, you don't have to worry about me. You can go and look for Aaron."

"Yah, I can." The sooner the better, it seemed. He

was doing no good, standing here, looking at her and longing for her.

"I'll set it up to leave tomorrow morning."

Maybe if he could repair the damage done to Aaron, well, maybe then he'd be free of the guilt that crippled him.

Chapter Fourteen

Once Lige was settled in bed that night, Rebecca gathered her writing materials and settled down at the kitchen table in the grossdaadi haus. Mamm and Daad were in the living room, and she could hear their soft tones without distinguishing their words.

A comforting sound, she decided. She remembered drifting off to sleep in the farmhouse as a child, hearing the low murmur of voices from downstairs. She'd always felt so safe when she heard it, knowing that Mamm and Daadi were near at hand. It had been her image of what marriage was, that quiet communication between two people who loved and cared for each other and their children.

Perhaps Lige was beginning to feel that, as well. She hoped so. He needed that sense of safety and stability in his life, and she was finally able to provide it.

For a time, she'd almost begun to believe that Daniel might be a part of that stability for Lige and for her. She'd done everything short of saying it outright today, and he hadn't responded. So that was a brief dream better forgotten.

Smoothing the tablet of writing paper in front of her, she tried to think how to begin. The words eluded her.

She heard a step behind her and turned to find Daadi there, watching her.

"What has put that frown on your face, Rebecca?" He rested his hand on her shoulder. "Is something amiss?"

"No, nothing." She closed the tablet, her first instinct to deny it and insist everything was fine.

Then she saw her father's face. He knew. Daadi always knew when one of his children was troubled. And it wasn't just the knowledge that stirred her. It was the hurt she saw there. Daadi was hurt because she was shutting him out.

The words she'd said to Daniel earlier seemed to mock her. She'd talked about learning to love again. To trust again. But she wasn't acting as if she'd learned that lesson very well, was she?

She let out a long breath and then pulled out the chair next to her as a silent invitation. Her father sat down, rested his elbows on the table and waited.

"It's John Mast," she said finally. "I still haven't heard from him. I haven't had a payment." She shook her head. "It seems silly, but I hadn't thought until today about how long it's been."

"Too long," Daadi said so promptly that he must have been thinking about it himself. "The money was due the week you arrived here. It was all very well to say he couldn't send it immediately, but how long does he expect you to wait?"

"I don't know." She toyed with the pen and writing pad in front of her. "I thought maybe I should write again and remind him, but it's hard to do that when it's family. I don't want to cause hard feelings."

Daad's reply was prompt. "Yah, it is difficult." He patted her hand. "But John Mast entered into a contract with you. It's not the action of an honest man to refuse to send his payment."

"I suppose he feels that since he's James's brother, I should give him whatever time he needs." She was surprised to find herself excusing him. "If he's had unexpected expenses this month…"

"Is that what he said in his letter?" Daadi interrupted her, which was a sign he'd been building up something he wanted to say.

"No," she admitted. The tone of that letter had been curt. "He didn't give any reason. Just said he'd send it when he could."

Daadi put his hand over hers, making her look at him. "That's not right, Rebecca, and you know it. If he were paying a mortgage to a bank, would he do that?"

"No, but when it's family…" Why she was defending John, she couldn't imagine. But she was anxious to be fair.

"All the more reason to meet his obligations," her father said firmly. "I think you know better, Rebecca. Would any Amish man see his brother's widow and child go without, even if there wasn't a matter of a contract? John is not behaving as he should."

The sternness in his face eased a little as he studied her face. "Ach, Rebecca, you are bending over to excuse John Mast because he is James's brother, but that isn't right. More, it's not gut for him. Your lenience is allowing him to move along a road that will harm him in the end."

She smiled involuntarily. "That's the way you raised us, ain't so? Knowing that our spiritual and moral growth depended on being taught to do right."

"And the way you are raising Lige, as well. John doesn't seem to have learned the importance of keeping his word. It would be wrong not to call him to account."

"That's what's been going through my mind today. Once I knew that Shannon was back and the baby safe, I felt…" She struggled to find the words, but they escaped her.

"You stood up for what you knew you should do, and you were proved right." He patted her hand. "Now you must do the same with John. You've already decided that in your own heart, ain't so?"

"I guess so." She picked up the pen. "Even if it causes hard feelings in the family, I must remind John of his responsibility."

Daadi smiled. "Remind him as well, that he signed a written contract. No need to threaten. Just a reminder will do."

"Thanks to you, we have a contract. He kept saying it was in the family and there was no need to put it in writing. I might have given in if you hadn't insisted."

"Maybe then you would have, when you were worn down by everything that had happened. But not now. Now you have your strength back." He pushed his chair back. "I'll leave you to get on with it."

She hesitated, and then she knew what she wanted. And what would please him.

"When I've written it, will you take a look at it before I send it?"

Daadi's smile warmed his lean face. "I would be

wonderful glad to, Rebecca." He went back to Mamm, looking as if she had given him a present.

She opened the pad and began to write, feeling the support of her family behind her with every word she put down. This was the way it should be in a family— all of them giving and receiving help and love in equal measure.

"The stables should be just ahead." Dave Smith, Daniel's driver, leaned forward to peer at a road sign. The retired truck driver seemed as fresh as could be after all those hours behind the wheel.

Daniel decided Dave must be used to it. He couldn't say the same for himself, though. His muscles were stiff with the inactivity, and he'd begun to feel that if he couldn't get away from the radio Dave played constantly, his head might explode. How did people stand having that artificial noise constantly in their ears?

A long, low stable appeared on their left, and Daniel's stomach lurched. That was the place. Now, if only his brother were working today...

A nightmarish thought rushed into his mind. What if Aaron had left? What if he were on vacation or away on business or even having the day off?

Then he'd wait. Or he'd follow Aaron, wherever he'd gone. He hadn't come all this way to be balked at now.

Dave pulled up next to the stable, and Daniel saw now that another row of stalls lay beyond this one. All around were paddocks and training grounds, and the oval of a track showed between the buildings.

"Big operation," Dave muttered, looking around

before giving Daniel a sideways glance. "I hope you find him."

Nodding his thanks, Daniel got out slowly. He stretched, not hurrying, just thinking it over in his mind. He'd had plenty of time to figure out what he was going to say to his brother. In fact, in the middle of the night, he'd been very eloquent.

Now his mind was numb and his tongue felt paralyzed. He'd be fortunate if he could say anything at all once he came face to face with Aaron. He started walking toward the nearest door. *This is a mistake. He'll be angry. It will backfire, and he'll never want to speak to you again.*

Rebecca's concerned face appeared in his mind, chasing away the dark thoughts. He tried to repeat her words, as best he could remember them. She'd needed to know that home was still waiting for her. That people still loved her there. That was the gist of it, if not the exact words.

Maybe that was something Aaron needed to hear, as well. He hadn't found a way to say it in a letter, so he'd have to try it in person. Surely, just to see his brother's face again would make the trip worthwhile, even if that were all he had.

An older man in jeans and a flannel shirt was shoveling a stall just inside the door. He gave Daniel an incurious glance and then looked again, taking in the black pants and the straw hat he wore.

He leaned on the stall door. "Help you?"

Daniel took a deep breath. "I'm looking for Aaron King. I heard he worked here."

The man studied him for a moment longer and then

shrugged. "Through that door at the end. He's got a two-year-old out in the paddock."

"Thank you." He kept himself carefully to Englisch, suspecting the man wouldn't know anything else.

He walked on, wondering. It hadn't occurred to him to think that Aaron might not want his friends here to know he was Amish. But it was possible. He knew that some young men who left tried hard to forget everything about being Amish. Seemed like the further away they got, the better, as far as they were concerned.

Funny how that worked. Some folks right in his own church district had kin that had jumped the fence, but they still had good relationships with them. Like Sarah and Luke Bitler, whose Englisch grandchildren came to spend every summer with them.

But it seemed Aaron hadn't been one of those. When he'd left, he'd cut off all ties. Thinking of the years when they hadn't known if he was dead or alive, Daniel felt a wave of bitterness and regret. They couldn't go back to that at least. Now they did know he was alive.

And working with horses—always his first love. There he was, working a young horse at the end of a long line, snapping a buggy whip in the air to signal the animal. Daniel moved closer, content to feast his eyes on his little brother at last.

Not so little, that was certain. Aaron was taller than he was, with a lean, rugged strength that handled both the line and the whip effortlessly. His hair had darkened, but it was still a lighter brown than either his or Caleb's. He wore jeans and a flannel shirt, like the other man, with brown leather boots that made Daniel think of a cowboy.

Aaron, turning in a circle as he worked the animal, caught sight of Daniel. His face expressed nothing—not welcome or anger. Just…nothing but a tightness so hard he might have been carved from stone.

Daniel's heart caught. What made him look so hard? It couldn't just be the sight of his brother. He'd already worn that expression before he even noticed Daniel.

Ignoring him, Aaron focused on the horse, slowing him down from a trot to a walk, shortening the rope until the animal came to a halt in front of him. Holding the halter, Aaron crossed the paddock to him, stopping a couple of feet away and looping the rope over the fence.

"So," he said at last. "I should have known Eli would talk. He never could keep anything to himself."

"Don't blame him." Daniel kept his tone easy with an effort, sensing he had to be as gentle with his brother as Aaron would be with an untrained colt. "His wife made him do it."

Something that might have been a smile tugged at Aaron's mouth. "Guess that would happen. Who'd he marry?"

"Esther Stoltzfus. You remember her from school?"

Aaron nodded. "Bossy."

There was nothing much to say to that, since it was a fine description of Esther.

Aaron picked up a towel from an equipment caddy that sat on the ground by the fence. "I've got to get back to work. What do you want, Daniel?"

Daniel ducked between the rails and picked up

another cloth, starting to wipe down the other side of the horse. The two-year-old rolled his eyes toward Daniel and then seemed to decide not to protest.

"Wanted to see how my little brother is doing," he said. "Not so little anymore, yah?"

He'd switched to Pennsylvania Dutch without thinking of it when he'd seen Aaron, and his brother had answered him in dialect, too. So at least he hadn't forgotten the language of his family.

"Bigger than you anyway." He seemed to focus on the horse, but finally he glanced at Daniel and then away. "How's the family?"

Daniel breathed a silent prayer of mingled gratitude and longing. "Caleb is fine. Broke his leg pretty badly a while back, but it's healed okay, so he's back to running the dairy farm. That gives me time to devote to my carpentry business. He's married again now. Jessie's a fine woman and wonderful gut with the kinder. And they're growing like weeds."

"And Onkel Zeb?"

Was that anxiety in his voice? Would he be grieving if something had happened to the old man since he'd been gone?

"Zeb's the same as ever. He gets up before dawn for the milking, and he puts in a full day of work. Sometimes we have to trick him to get him to take a rest."

Aaron didn't respond, but Daniel thought his expression eased a bit. "You're not married, I see."

Daniel brushed a hand along his beardless face, trying not to think of Rebecca. "I run too fast," he said lightly.

Silence again, and he sought for something to say to keep Aaron talking.

"Looks like quite an operation here. You doing the training, are you?"

Aaron gave a short nod. "It's sulky racing mostly around here. The boss breeds them and sometimes picks up likely youngsters at the auctions. I go along to help out with that."

"You were always gut at judging horseflesh."

Aaron shrugged, not volunteering anything else.

"Are you satisfied here?" He didn't ask if Aaron was happy. It certain sure wasn't happiness that had given him a face like a stone.

"It's okay. As long as I can work with the horses, that's good enough."

"Plenty of horses to work with back in Lost Creek," he ventured.

Aaron's body become taut, as if every muscle stilled. Then he tossed the curry brush in the caddy. He grasped the horse's halter, untying the rope. "I'd better get back to work." He didn't look at Daniel as he opened the gate and led the horse through.

Daniel followed, feeling his chances slipping away. On impulse, he reached out to grasp his brother's shoulder. The muscles felt like iron under his hand, but Aaron didn't pull away.

"Now that we've found you, we don't want to lose touch. Just let us know you're well from time to time. Please."

"I've got a new life now." He muttered the words, not looking at Daniel. Then he stepped away, so that Daniel's hand fell from his shoulder.

"Yah, we know. We respect that." He hesitated, but he had to say it. It was what he'd come to say. "But the farm is always home for you, if you ever want it. We will always love you and want you."

For an instant, he thought Aaron would fling away from him. Instead, he stood, his face working as if he struggled to contain it.

Finally he spoke. "Denke." His voice was gruff. "Goodbye, Daniel."

Daniel waited for a moment, hoping for more. For Aaron, ramrod straight, walked away.

Daniel looked down at the hand that had touched his brother after all this time. For a moment, they had been connected. He had longed to grab Aaron—to pull him into his arms.

But it would have been a mistake. If Aaron came back, it had to be because he wanted to, not because Daniel had pushed and manipulated him.

His thoughts lifted in a silent prayer for his brother as he walked slowly toward the car. He might have little to show for this visit, but he would never regret it.

Chapter Fifteen

Rebecca, getting ready to leave for the shop on Monday morning, was trying not to wonder what happened with Daniel and Aaron. Unfortunately, trying didn't seem to be enough to keep the subject from her mind. *When would she know?*

Leah glanced at her from the counter where she was kneading bread dough. "I saw Daniel got back from his trip last night. I hope things went well with Aaron."

Everyone seemed to know the purpose of Daniel's trip. That was inevitable in the close-knit Amish community. Some folks probably thought it a foolish errand, but most would have prayed for him. And for Aaron.

No member of the Leit wanted to lose one of their own, and since Aaron hadn't been baptized into the church, he could still return, confess and slip into his place, as if he'd never been gone. The church would close around him, and the community would be whole again.

"Yah, I hope so, too." What else could she say?

The weight of the part she'd played in his decision pressed on her.

"Have you heard how it went?" Apparently not satisfied, Leah resorted to a direct question.

Rebecca managed a smile at her tactics. "If I knew, I would tell you, but I haven't talked to him yet. And even when I see him, I don't know that he'll want to talk about it."

"As close as you are, surely he'll confide in you." Leah gave the smooth mound of dough a pat, as if she were patting a baby, and turned around, wiping her hands on a towel. "You and he were always close, ain't so?"

"That was a long time ago." She tried to speak lightly, but it was difficult when her heart was yearning to help Daniel.

"Not so long." She fell silent and then shook her head slightly. "Ach, I can't do it. Sam would tell me to keep silent, but I can't, not when I see you hurting so much. I want to see you and Daniel as happy as Sam and I are. You two belong together. You always have."

Rebecca would like to believe that, but she couldn't. "Maybe, once, it would have worked out. But when I went away, Daniel still looked on me as a friend, nothing more."

"Daniel was as foolish as most boys were at that age," Leah said tartly. "He'd have grown out of chasing after other girls in time. He'd have realized that his true friend was also his true love."

"We'll never know, ain't so? I didn't wait. I rushed into marrying, and now it's too late." Her marriage to James would have ended any chance for her and Daniel, even if Daniel's stubborn insistence on bearing guilt that was not his own had not existed. But she had Lige, and she could never regret the choices that had given him to her.

Leah looked as if she'd like to argue. Then, pressing her lips together, she came to Rebecca and hugged her. "You deserve your happiness," she said softly. "And so does Daniel."

Rebecca hugged her back, comforted. "Perhaps. But we must be satisfied with what the Lord sends us."

She pulled away, gathering up what she'd need for the day. She would stop thinking about being anything else to Daniel and focus on being his friend. Whatever had happened with Aaron, he needed a friend now.

To Rebecca's surprise, when she reached the shop, Daniel was already there. The kitchen looked like a construction zone, with the old cabinets gone and one of the new ones Daniel had been making set up on a pair of sawhorses.

"I didn't expect you—" she began and then stopped, startled. "What happened to the refrigerator?"

Daniel looked surprised, as well. "Didn't you know? Your daad came in first thing this morning. He traded it in for a gas one. He said the store was bringing a new gas refrigerator to the daadi haus and moving that one in here."

"But he didn't say a word to me about it." She couldn't decide whether she was upset or thankful. Maybe a little of both. "I wish he wouldn't do things like that. I'm sure Mamm didn't think she needed a new one. It's just an excuse to get one put in for me."

Daniel didn't go so far as to chuckle, but there was laughter in his eyes. "I don't think you're ever going to outfox him. And I bet, if you ask her, your mamm will say she loves her new refrigerator."

"She'll agree with him, that's certain sure. I just don't want him spending money on me."

"I thought you were going to let him help you. Isn't that what you were telling me?"

"I know." She felt herself flush. "But even so... well, if John comes through with the money he owes, I can pay him back."

"I doubt you can get him to take it." Daniel seemed to be clearing a path to the spot for the new refrigerator. "Have you some reason to think your brother-in-law has come to his senses?"

She probably shouldn't let him talk that way about John, but the trouble was that she thought the same. "Not yet, but I wrote to him a few days ago." She still got a little queasy feeling in her stomach when she thought about it. "Daad and I agreed that he needed a reminder of the contract he signed. I hope that's all he needs. It was hard enough to make myself go that far."

"But you did." He was studying her with what seemed to be approval. "I'm glad to see you're getting your spunk back."

"I don't know about that." She smiled at the word. "But I guess everything that's happened has given me some courage—opening the shop, dealing with that business over Shannon. I feel like I can cope with things now."

"You can," Daniel said, his voice firm. "You always could. Your confidence just got a little dented there for a while."

She ducked her head, not sure what to say. Then it

struck her that Daniel might well be keeping the talk on her because he didn't want to tell her about Aaron.

If so, shouldn't she respect that? Or was it the part of a friend to encourage him to open up about what happened?

In the momentary pause, Daniel bent to pick up a hammer. Then he just stood there, staring at it, as if he didn't remember what he'd intended to do with it.

"You…you had a long drive." A hopeless way to start, but all that came out of her mouth.

"Yah." He was still studying the hammer. Finally he put it down and looked at her. "I guess you want to know what happened."

"Only if you want to tell me." She took a step closer, wishing she knew how to make this easier.

"Well, I saw him." He gave her a fleeting smile. "My little bruder is all grown-up."

"I guess he would be," she said, trying not to sound too eager. "How did he look?"

"Okay, I guess. Englisch." He grimaced slightly, making her long to comfort him.

"That would be hard." How would she feel if Sam had left, or one of her other brothers? How would it be to see him after all that time, looking like a stranger?

"It's funny, but it wasn't as odd as it seems. I knew he'd have changed, but when I saw him working with a young horse, it was just like watching the old Aaron. You know how he was with the horses."

She nodded, remembering. "I remember Daadi saying that Aaron was born able to talk to the horses. It's a gift, ain't so?"

"Yah. And at least that hasn't changed. He acted like he was satisfied with his job there."

It seemed to Rebecca that Daniel was making an effort to talk about it without letting his emotions run free. Maybe he was afraid of what he'd say if he let go.

"Was he…was he happy being Englisch? Does he have friends? People he can count on?"

Daniel shrugged. "How can I say? We only talked for a few minutes. By his choice, not mine."

He sounded annoyed, and it was probably better to let him take his frustration out on her than on himself. If she knew him, he was already blaming himself still more.

"I'm sorry. I wish you could have had more time with him."

"No, I'm the one to be sorry." He gave her a sideways, sheepish look. "It's not your fault. I wish that, as well."

"You were disappointed."

"No, not exactly. At least I saw him. I did ask him to let us know from time to time that he's all right." He seemed to turn that over in his mind. "You know, now that I go back over it, I think he was almost surprised to hear that we still think of him and want him back."

"I'd say that if you succeeded in doing that, you've done a lot for one short visit, ain't so?" She held her breath. Was he going to explode at that idea?

Instead, he looked as if he were actually considering her words. "You might be right. If you'd asked me what I expected from the visit beforehand, I'd have said I'd be content just to see he was all right." He gave a wry smile. "We're always expecting more from the Father, aren't we? Thinking that He will give us what we want in exchange for very little effort on our part."

She turned that over in her mind. Had she sometimes expected that result from her prayers? Thinking that God might swoop in and solve her problems? Probably so.

"Are you disappointed then?" She held her breath for the answer, fearing the increased pain he'd feel if he thought he'd failed his brother again.

For an instant, Daniel looked surprised. "No, I guess I'm not," he said slowly, as if he were thinking it through. "At least I saw Aaron. I told him what I wanted him to hear—that we loved and missed him and wanted him back. But Onkel Zeb was right, too. Aaron is a grown man now. He has to decide for himself what he wants."

Rebecca felt able to breathe again. He was taking this better, more sensibly, than she'd have dared hope. "You did all you could," she said.

Daniel nodded, and his face wore an expression of peace she'd never seen before when he talked about his brother. "I opened the door. I will pray he walks through it, but that he has to do on his own."

Once they had separated, each going to work on the day's project, Rebecca lifted her heart in prayers of thanksgiving. God had given Daniel release from some of the grief and regret that bound him. She could only hope and dream that he would move the rest of the way to healing.

Rebecca busied herself by cutting the five-inch squares of quilting fabrics several of her customers had asked for. Apparently, a lot of quilters found it made more sense to buy the squares already cut than to buy fabric by the yard and perhaps waste some.

Not that she'd ever found it a waste. The leftover

material could always be used for something, she'd found. Still, she was in business to provide what her customers wanted, and if they were willing to pay a little more for precut squares, she was happy to oblige them.

One of the Englisch women who'd come to the shop had even said she'd bought precut squares through the internet. It seemed strange to Rebecca to buy fabric when you couldn't see it or feel it in your hands, but apparently it was so.

The work kept her hands occupied and left her mind free to wander. It went, as it so often did recently, to the changes she saw in herself since she'd returned to Lost Creek. What a pitiful creature she'd been—tied up in knots and blaming herself, afraid even to trust and rely on those who loved her best. Being here had healed her.

Or rather, the good Lord had healed her, working through those around her. Even someone like Lydia Schultz, with her gossipy tongue, had contributed, showing Rebecca that she was becoming strong again.

Most of all, always there, so necessary to her happiness, there was Daniel. For so long, she hadn't even recognized that she was learning to love him in a new way. She hadn't seen it until it was too late to prevent it. She couldn't stop loving him, even if he never made a move toward her.

Those moments when Daniel had responded to her…she hadn't imagined them. He had feelings for her. She was sure of it. But if he never allowed himself to recognize those feelings…

Footsteps sounded on the porch, and even as she looked up, the door opened, bell jingling wildly. A man strode in. Not just any man. John Mast, James's brother.

The scissors dropped from her suddenly nerveless fingers as she struggled for control. That letter. He must have come in response to her letter.

"John." She forced herself to sound cordial, forced her stiff lips to smile. "I wasn't expecting you. Wilkom."

His face was set in lines so harsh they seemed engraved into his skin. He stalked to the counter, and his expression had her taking an involuntary step back.

No. She would not be that person again. Just because John looked like James in one of his rages, she could not let herself cower. She was over that.

But her throat was dry, and her stomach had clenched into a knot.

John slammed something down on the counter. Her letter.

"I came because of that." His voice was loud, like his brother's when he was angry.

Rebecca grasped the edge of the counter, trying to quell the trembling inside her, and sent a silent plea flying in prayer. *Please, Lord. Help me.*

Finding himself at a momentary standstill in the kitchen until the new refrigerator arrived, Daniel had gone upstairs to check out what was needed there. The room at the front of the house, over the shop, was the largest, plainly intended to be a master bedroom. It actually had an adjoining bathroom, which the last owners had installed.

The wooden planks of the floor were in pretty good condition, but they'd need to be either refinished or painted. He took a step and found one that creaked and gave under his foot. Frowning, he knelt to check it out.

He was kneeling there when he heard the slam of the shop door. His eyebrows lifted. The ladies who came to the quilt shop were not usually quite so noisy. Motionless, he listened for any sound from below.

A few minutes later he could have heard clearly without any need for kneeling. The voice of the man who'd entered the shop carried clearly. It didn't take much thinking to realize this was Rebecca's brother-in-law. She had written to him to remind him to pay, and it sounded as if he'd come to deliver his response in person.

The loud, bullying tones set his teeth on edge, and his hands curled involuntarily into fists. Daniel forced them to relax. That wasn't the Amish way of solving problems, but if anyone deserved to be forcibly reminded of his manners, it must surely be John Mast.

A human being could only take so much. Daniel surged to his feel and went quickly out of the room and down the stairs, his thoughts forced on Rebecca. How was she coping?

A second later, that thought fled, because of what he saw. Lige was at the foot of the stairs. He'd curled his small body into a ball, so that Daniel couldn't see his face. But he could see the way he was trembling, his hands clamped to his ears.

Focused on the boy, he reached the bottom of the steps and spoke softly. "Lige, it's all right. It's Daniel. Can you look at me?"

There was no movement at first, and he feared the boy had retreated beyond his reach. But finally Lige raised his head enough for Daniel to see his white tearstained face. Daniel's heart wrenched as if a fist had grabbed it.

"It's all right," he said again. He opened his arms, and Lige bolted into them. The boy wrapped his arms around Daniel's neck and buried his face in Daniel's shoulder.

Daniel scooped him up and carried him quickly to the back porch. It hurt to walk away from Rebecca, but it sounded as if she was holding her own. Lige needed help now.

Setting the boy down, he knelt beside him, tipping his face up gently. "It scared you, ain't so? Hearing your onkel that way."

Lige nodded. "It…it sounded like Daadi," he whispered, lowering his face again.

Daniel's heart winced. "It's not, but we can't let him talk that way to your mammi. So I'm going to go in there, and I want you to run to the farmhouse and tell Grossdaadi what's happening. Can you do that?"

The small face suddenly looked up at Daniel's. "But Mammi…" he whispered.

"I'll take care of Mammi. I need you to be brave now and run as fast as you can. Okay?"

Lige hesitated, his huge blue eyes fixated on Daniel's face. Finally he nodded. He turned and spurted off the porch as if he'd been shot from a gun, running toward the farmhouse with all his might.

Lige had trusted him. The thought overwhelmed him. Lige trusted him to know what was right and do it.

Daniel walked quickly through the house, toward the shop. Rebecca might not feel the same way Lige did. She'd expressed, again and again, her need to handle things on her own. She'd probably be ready to tear a strip off him for interfering.

But no matter how angry it made her, he couldn't stop. The people who loved her had the right to stand beside her in times of trouble. He did.

There was no time to analyze that thought. He pushed the door open and went into the shop.

Rebecca and her brother-in-law stood facing each other on either side of the counter, at the front of the shop. Mast seemed to loom over Rebecca, and it sounded as if he was hectoring her to change the terms of the contract.

As for Rebecca…her pallor smote his heart, but in spite of that, she stood erect, her shoulders back. Her voice was so soft in comparison to the man's that he couldn't quite make out her words.

Forcing down his anger, he went to them, his movement drawing Mast's attention. He glowered as Daniel moved to stand behind Rebecca. She didn't speak or turn, but she took a half step closer to him, and he could almost feel her gratitude reaching out to him.

Mast glared at him. "This is a private conversation."

"Daniel is my friend." Rebecca spoke firmly, her voice sounding louder, more certain. "I have no objection to his being here. What I have to say is simple. You signed a contract, and you will have to honor it."

Mast's face darkened. "It's not right. That property belonged to my brother. He'd have wanted me to farm it. You had no right to sell it away from the family."

"I didn't. I sold it to you." She put a faint stress on the word sold.

Mast glanced from Rebecca to Daniel and seemed

to make an effort to switch his ground. "You'll get your money. Just because I happened to be a little short this month is no reason for you to make a fuss."

For a moment, Daniel feared Rebecca would waver. She'd stood up against anger, but an appeal was something different. He prayed she wasn't going to let her soft heart betray her. He probably shouldn't speak, but the words were out before he could stop them.

"Your brother's son shouldn't have to suffer for your financial problems. You signed an agreement."

Rebecca shot him a look, but he didn't have time to reassure her. Obviously, he'd infuriated Mast.

"It's not your business." He glared at Daniel and then shifted back to Rebecca. "I'll pay when I'm ready and not before. You're not going to sue your own brother-in-law, and there's nothing else you can do, contract or no contract."

Silence greeted his ultimatum. Maybe he'd guessed correctly. Rebecca would be reluctant to go that far, and his hands were tied.

"If you refuse to pay what is owed, I will help my daughter take you to court."

Rebecca's father came toward them, with Sam right behind him. The old man's face was stern and calm, but Sam looked as if he were having difficulty containing himself. Behind them, Lige slid in, moving like a shadow to Daniel's side.

Daniel put his hand on the boy's shoulder, and they stood together.

Mast hesitated, his confidence seeming to dip for the first time. "You wouldn't do that. Amish don't sue other Amish."

"I would rather not, but I don't really think that will

be necessary." All of Rebecca's strength must have come back now, and she seemed to know just what to say. "I will speak to your parents first. I don't think they want to see their grandson cheated of what is his. And if that doesn't work, I'll speak to the bishop. You will meet your obligations, John."

Daniel nearly smiled at the baffled expression on the man's face. He'd clearly expected to have no difficulty in cowing Rebecca into agreeing with him, and he didn't know what to do with the Rebecca who faced him down. She was a different person from the one he'd known in Ohio.

With a sudden movement, he slapped a wad of cash down on the counter. Without a word, he turned and lumbered out of the shop.

For a long moment, there was silence. Maybe they were all waiting to hear the driver who'd brought John leaving. When the sound of the car turning out onto the road came, Rebecca took a deep breath.

She turned and looked from one to another of them. "Denke," she said softly. "Thank you for standing with me."

Chapter Sixteen

Daniel felt oddly flat that evening after his happiness at the successful conclusion of Rebecca's business with her brother-in-law. *Why?* He frowned at the cabinet he was making for Rebecca's kitchen, but it had no answers.

What was he regretting? Rebecca had obviously not held it against him that he'd intervened and that he'd sent for her father. He should be happy. Her response had told all of them that she'd regained what she'd lost in her marriage to James. She was not the girl she'd been, but she was the woman she'd been intended to become.

Onkel Zeb came in, interrupting his musing, and he attempted to look busy. Zeb, next to him, ran his hand along the curve of the cabinet door.

"Fine piece of work. It's for Rebecca's kitchen, ain't so?"

He nodded, smiling a little. "It's a surprise, so don't say anything. It'll fit right into that corner by the refrigerator, and it's just deep enough to store some of her canned goods, nice and handy."

"Special built, just for her kitchen." Onkel Zeb studied his face. "A gift of love, you might say."

He supposed it was, but he certain sure didn't want to be that obvious. "I saw one like it in an Englisch kitchen, that's all. Thought it was a gut idea, and Rebecca should have one. Maybe I'll put them in all the kitchens I do."

"Maybe," his uncle agreed. "But only this one is what I said—a gift of love."

"Onkel Zeb…" he began, but he didn't get any further.

"Ach, don't bother denying it. Not to me. Do you think I don't know you any better than that after being around your whole life? You love Rebecca. So why aren't you doing something about it instead of hiding in your shop?"

"I'm not hiding," he was momentarily indignant. "I'm doing my job."

"Hiding," Zeb said firmly.

Daniel frowned at him, but Zeb's wise old eyes merely looked amused.

"All right," he said, capitulating. "Yah, if you must know, I…I have feelings for Rebecca."

"The whole county knows that. But have you told her so?" His uncle was clearly not letting this go.

The answer to that was evident, he supposed. "It's too soon. It hasn't been that long since her husband passed."

"And small loss to anyone, if half what I've heard is true. That's no reason for not telling her what you feel. Even if it is too soon to expect her to marry you all in a rush. Still, from what I can remember, no woman objects to being told she's loved."

Daniel glared at his uncle, who was unperturbed. "There's Lige to consider, too. I don't want to rush either of them. Is that all right with you?"

"Ach, Daniel, I've seen you with the boy. It's clear that he loves you and trusts you. He relies on you, and so does Rebecca. Can't you see that the two of you were made for each other? Everyone else can."

His uncle was awfully good at disposing of his reasons, but there was one he couldn't deny.

"Our family hasn't had much success with women. Maybe I…"

Zeb put a hand on his shoulder, giving him a light shake. "Don't talk that way. Your mamm hurt all of you when she left, but that's no reason to hide from love. Look how happy Caleb and Jessie are. And my Mary—even though we had just two short years, she made me happier than anyone else could in a lifetime."

His throat tightened. "I'm sorry. I didn't mean anything about you. It's me. What if…I make promises to them, and then I let them down?"

The hand on his shoulder squeezed tight for an instant. "Daniel, Daniel. Always so conscientious. Always blaming yourself when things go wrong. But that's foolishness. We can't control everything that happens in life, even for those we love the most. We can only love them, do our best and trust the Lord for everything else."

The message wasn't new, but the way his heart responded when he heard it was. He thought it would leap out of his chest. Onkel Zeb was right. Why was he wasting time when he had a chance at a love like Rebecca?

Onkel Zeb must have sensed the change in him,

because he smiled. He gave Daniel a gentle push toward the door. "Go on. Go to Rebecca. Right now."

Daniel's first few steps were tentative, dragged at by doubts. And then they fell away, and he was running across the field. He looked like a madman, and he didn't care. He had to see Rebecca.

Rebecca was sitting in the living room of the farmhouse with Leah and Mamm that evening, and they were all focused on a basketful of mending. Daadi was in the daadi haus with Lige, and as Mamm said, mending was more enjoyable when they made a work frolic out of it. Their conversation flowed easily as they worked, with the companionship of women who knew each other so well that words weren't always needed.

She heard the back door close, and in a moment, Sam appeared in the doorway, a smile teasing the corners of his mouth.

"Somebody to see you, Rebecca. Out on the back porch."

Putting her needle in the patch she was sewing, she rose. Surely John hadn't returned for another try. But no, Sam would hardly look amused at that. "Who is it?"

He gave her a gentle push. "It's Daniel. Seems to be something important, by the looks of him."

Rebecca eyed her brother suspiciously. "If you're trying to play a joke on me, it's not funny."

"It's no joke." Putting his arm around her waist, he propelled her across the room. "Go and put the poor man out of his misery."

She pulled herself free and frowned at him, but

her heart had begun thudding in her chest. "I suppose you think you're funny. Go find something to do with yourself."

Her knees showed a sudden tendency to shake, but she forced herself to walk steadily out to the porch. Daniel spun toward her at the movement of the door.

"Rebecca." For a moment, it seemed all he wanted was to look at her. Then he held out his hand. "Will you take a walk with me?"

She nodded, hardly daring to hope. They walked in silence along the lane and past the barn. When they reached the drooping branches of the old weeping willow by the pond, Daniel paused.

"Do you remember when you had a hideout under the branches of the willow?" He smiled down at her, but his eyes were dark and serious.

"I remember. I went there when I wanted to get away from Sam's teasing."

"It might still be a fine place to get away from anyone watching."

"Is someone watching?" He was facing toward the house, but she wasn't, and she wouldn't give anyone the satisfaction of looking.

His smile widened. "There's a face at every window."

Rebecca parted the long fronds of the willow stems, inviting him with a glance. They stepped inside, and the drooping branches fell back into place, enclosing them in a leafy green cave, with just enough light from the setting sun to see each other.

She waited. It was Daniel who'd come to her, so he had to speak first.

He seemed to have trouble getting started, clearing

his throat a couple of times. "I...I hope you're not angry with me for sending for your father earlier."

Rebecca had a sense that he had intended to say something different. She had to pause, adjusting her thoughts. Of course he might feel she'd be upset about his interference, since she'd so loudly proclaimed her ability to stand on her own feet.

"You do know I've got past that feeling, don't you? Especially when you've helped me with it so much." *And confided in me. And let me confide in you. That means something, doesn't it?*

"That's...that's gut. You have your confidence back. You can do anything."

"Not anything." She suspected she'd have to help him, or he'd never get to what he wanted to say. "I can't start a new family. Not by myself."

His lips twitched a little. "Rebecca, are you asking me?"

"No, I'm trying to encourage you to do the asking."

Daniel reached out and touched her face. Such a light, gentle touch, but it seemed to go straight to her heart.

"I have longed so much to tell you what I feel." His gaze held hers, drawing her closer and closer. "I've been afraid—afraid of letting you down, afraid of hurting Lige, maybe even afraid of myself."

Sure now, she put her hand over his, pressing his palm against her cheek. "So foolish," she murmured. "You don't have it in you to hurt either of us."

"No. I knew that when I heard John berating you today. When I went and stood with you. I didn't even think. I just did it because that was where I belonged. Because love means standing together at times like that." There was a light in his eyes, like a tiny flame flickering with his love for her.

"I know. I felt you there, and I wasn't afraid."

"My Rebecca. We belong together. Will you be my wife?"

Rebecca lifted her face to his. "I will."

She pronounced the words solemnly. It was a vow, a solemn promise before God. A recognition that the past was gone and a new future lay ahead for both of them.

Daniel leaned closer. His hand slid from her cheek to the back of her neck, spreading warmth everywhere he touched. He tilted her head so that their faces were very close—close enough that she could smell the honest male scent of him, close enough that his breath caressed her skin, making her tingle.

With a little sigh, she moved into his embrace. Daniel's lips met hers, sweet and gentle and filled with love. Rebecca knew, with his kiss, that the last faint vestige of pain was gone from her heart. Her arms slid around him, feeling the strong, flat muscles of his back, and she gave herself to his embrace.

Through all the dizziness and joy, Rebecca felt the truth that filled her heart. God was giving both of them a second chance to make the right choices. A chance to have a lifetime of happiness, a life that grew from two children playing together to a man and a woman who belong to each other, no matter what life brings.

Her heart overflowed with joy. They were both where they belonged at last.

* * * * *

*If you enjoyed this story,
don't miss the first book in the*
BRIDES OF LOST CREEK *series
from Marta Perry:*

SECOND CHANCE AMISH BRIDE

And be sure to pick up
AMISH CHRISTMAS BLESSINGS *from
Love Inspired,
featuring Marta Perry's*
THE MIDWIFE'S CHRISTMAS SURPRISE

Find more great reads at www.LoveInspired.com

Dear Reader,

I'm so happy you decided to pick up the second book in my Brides of Lost Creek series. I had such a good time visiting the Lost Creek Amish again for a new love story, and I hope you enjoyed reading it.

The new book captures the story of Daniel King, an Amish carpenter, who is determined to remain a bachelor. Daniel has what he feels are good reasons to stay away from a romantic involvement, but all of his ideas are put to the test when his childhood playmate Rebecca Mast returns to the farm next door after the death of her husband. Sorrow and pain have changed Rebecca drastically from the happy girl he knew, and he feels compelled to help her despite the danger that his childhood friend might become his forever love.

The Amish community of Lost Creek is based on several Amish groups here in central Pennsylvania, most of them daughter settlements to the Lancaster County Amish. They've settled here for the less expensive farmland and the welcoming environment. Most of my story ideas begin with a place, and I love it when I can write about my own home area, the place I love most.

Please let me know if you enjoyed my story. You can reach me via my website, www.martaperry.com, on my Facebook page, www.Facebook.com/martaperrybooks, and via email at marta@martaperry.com. I'd be happy to reply and to send you a signed bookmark and my brochure of Pennsylvania Dutch recipes.

All the best,

Marta Perry

Get 4 FREE REWARDS!

We'll send you 2 FREE Books plus 2 FREE Mystery Gifts.

Love Inspired® books feature contemporary inspirational romances with Christian characters facing the challenges of life and love.

FREE
Value Over
$20

SPECIAL EXCERPT FROM

Love Inspired®

*With his orphaned nephew depending on him, Amish
carpenter Eli Troyer moves to Harmony Creek Hollow
to start over. And when schoolteacher Miriam Hartz
offers to teach hearing-impaired Eli how to read lips, he
can't refuse. Given both of their pasts, dare they hope to
fit together as a family...forever?*

Read on for a sneak preview of
THE AMISH SUITOR by Jo Ann Brown,
available in June 2018 from Love Inspired!

"If you want, I can teach you to read lips."

"What?"

Miriam touched her lips and then raised and lowered
her fingers against her thumb as if they were a duck's bill.
"Talk. I can help you understand what people are saying
by watching them talk."

When he realized what Miriam was doing, Eli was
stunned. A nurse at the hospital where he'd woken
after the wall's collapse had suggested that, once he
was healed, he should learn to read lips. He'd pushed
that advice aside, because he didn't have time with the
obligations of his brother's farm and his brother's son.

During the past four years he and his nephew had
created a unique language together. Mostly Kyle had
taught it to him, helping him decipher the meaning and
context of the few words he could capture.

"How do you know about lipreading?" Eli asked.

LIEXP0518

"My *grossmammi*." She tapped one ear, then the other. "...hearing...as she grew older. We...together. We practiced together. I can help." She put her hands on Kyle's shoulders. "Kyle...grows up. Who will...you then?"

Who would help him when Kyle wasn't nearby? He was sure that was what she'd asked. It was a question he'd posed to himself more and more often as Kyle reached the age to start attending school.

Not for the first time, Eli thought about the burden he'd placed on Kyle. Though Eli was scrupulous in making time for Kyle to be a *kind*, sometimes, like when they went to a store, he found himself needing the little boy to confirm a total when he was checking out or to explain where to find something on the shelves. If he didn't agree to Miriam's help, he was condemning his nephew to a lifetime of having to help him.

"All right," Eli said. "You can try to teach me to read lips."

Miriam seemed so confident she could teach him. He didn't want to disappoint her when she was going out of her way to help him.

Kyle threw his arms around Miriam and gave her a big hug. He grinned, and Eli realized how eager the *kind* was to let someone else help Eli fill in the blanks.

Don't miss
THE AMISH SUITOR by Jo Ann Brown,
available June 2018 wherever
Love Inspired® books and ebooks are sold.

www.LoveInspired.com

Inspirational Romance to Warm Your Heart and Soul

Join our social communities to connect with other readers who share your love!

Sign up for the Love Inspired newsletter at **www.LoveInspired.com** to be the first to find out about upcoming titles, special promotions and exclusive content.

CONNECT WITH US AT:

Harlequin.com/Community

 Facebook.com/LoveInspiredBooks

 Twitter.com/LoveInspiredBks

LISOCIAL2017

Looking for inspiration in tales
of hope, faith and heartfelt romance?

Check out **Love Inspired**® and
Love Inspired® **Suspense** books!

New books available every month!

CONNECT WITH US AT:

Harlequin.com/Community

 Facebook.com/HarlequinBooks

 Twitter.com/HarlequinBooks

 Instagram.com/HarlequinBooks

 Pinterest.com/HarlequinBooks

ReaderService.com